and the Missing Misp

Poog

Akiko

Spuckler

Mr. Beeba

Gax

and the Missing Misp

Written and illustrated by
Mark Crilley

DELACORTE PRESS

Published by Delacorte Press
an imprint of Random House Children's Books
a division of Random House, Inc.
New York

www.randomhouse.com/kids

Educators and librarians, for a variety of teaching tools, visit us at
www.randomhouse.com/teachers

Library of Congress Cataloging-in-Publication Data
Crilley, Mark.
Akiko and the missing Misp / Mark Crilley.—1st ed.
p. cm.
Summary: Sixth-grader Akiko makes another visit to the planet Smoo, but on
the way she passes through a time warp that sends her back twenty-five years.
ISBN 978-0-385-73045-7 (hardcover)
[1. Adventure and adventurers—Fiction. 2. Life on other planets—Fiction.
3. Japanese Americans—Fiction. 4. Science fiction.] I. Title.
PZ7.C869275Afm 2008
[Fic]—dc22
2007037232

The text of this book is set in 14-point Hoefler New Roman.

Printed in the United States of America

10 9 8 7 6 5 4 3 2 1

First Edition

For my daughter, Mio

and the Missing Misp

Chapter 1

My name is Akiko. Every school has at least one daydreamer: A kid whose head is always in the clouds, picturing herself in some far-off magical place that doesn't really exist. A kid who is so good at seeing that imaginary world that she knows every last detail of it. A kid who spends so much of her day-to-day life sailing through the land of make-believe she can no longer tell the difference between fantasy and reality. I just want you all to know one thing.

I am not that kid.

Seriously. I couldn't come up with an amazing fantasy world to save my life. Plus, you know what? I don't have the energy for it.

There's just one problem. My real life *sounds* like something out of a fantasy world. It's got everything a good fantasy world needs: rocket ship rides to distant galaxies, floating purple aliens, laser beams, lither serpents, you name it.

But the thing is, it's all real. It's really, truly, absolutely, 101 percent real. I swear.

So please keep that firmly in mind as I tell you the following story. Every time you want to say "Oh, come on," or "Gimme a break," or "What kind of fool do you take me for?" just bite your lip and read on. Because to you it may sound like the most unbelievable tall tale you've ever heard. But to me . . . well, it's just something that happened last Wednesday afternoon.

I was at the Middleton Convention Center, attending the First Annual Middleton Mega MangaFest with one of my very closest friends, Elizabeth Seto. The two of us had created our own manga at the local copy shop: *The Hard-to-Believe (But Nonetheless*

True) Adventures of Buckler Spoach and His Remarkable Robot, Grax. I was the writer—okay, you probably guessed that from the title—and Elizabeth was the illustrator.

Elizabeth is flat-out the best artist at Middleton Elementary—she drew Pokémon characters so well back in the fourth grade that kids at school fell all over themselves trying to get her to sell them. So I felt *very* lucky to have her doing all the pictures for our project. I mean, the drawings she did of Grax were spectacular: you could see every loose bolt and every spot of rust. And the spread of Buckler's ranch was so realistic that I swear you could almost smell the Blotka burgers sizzling on the grill. So you'd have thought we'd have people lining up around the block to buy our manga and have it signed by Elizabeth and me.

Sadly, this "Mega MangaFest" was about as *un*-mega as you could get, and the manga *creators* outnumbered the manga *buyers* by about fifty to one. The only attention Elizabeth and I were getting was from the mosquitoes that kept buzzing in through the propped-open door behind our table.

SMAK!

"Rrgh!" I leaned down and examined my calf. "They're eating me alive. Now I'll be scratching myself for the rest of the day."

"Oh no, you won't." Elizabeth turned away from me and fiddled with something in her purse. She then turned back to me with a mock-serious expression. "I shall stop the itching."

I smiled. Elizabeth's family was Chinese and her father was a doctor, so we had this running joke about her having been born with magical healing powers.

"I shall stop the itching with the ancient Chinese medicinal art of dim sum."

I peered at her from beneath half-closed eyelids. "Elizabeth. You and I both know that dim sum is *not* a medicinal art. . . ."

"You dare to doubt Seto the Great?" Elizabeth

deepened her voice and did her best Darth Vader impression (which was actually pretty darned good): "I find your lack of faith disturbing."

"Okay, okay." I raised my hands in surrender. "Dim sum me. If it stops the itching, I'm a believer."

Elizabeth got down on one knee and rubbed her fingers on my calf. My skin soon grew tingly and warm. If I were just a tiny bit more gullible, I'd have been a believer indeed.

"Okay, what did you put on your fingers? Come on."

"I'm telling you, it's the art of dim sum." Elizabeth then grinned and pulled a little glass bottle from her purse. "And this. *Bai Hua You*. White flower oil. Best thing for mosquito bites you'll ever find." She twisted the tiny blue cap on good and tight and handed me the bottle. "Go ahead and keep it. We've got loads back home."

I stuck the bottle in my pocket and did an exaggeratedly worshipful bow toward Elizabeth.

"O great and magical Elizabeth. You have saved me from the evil bloodsucking beasts of Mos Quito. I am your obedient disciple now and will follow you everywhere you go, including the bathroom."

Elizabeth laughed. "Now I'm starting to find your *presence* of faith a little disturbing."

Only then did I realize a girl had been standing in front of our table for who knew how long.

"Hi!" I fairly shouted, fearing that we might never have another shot at a customer again. "Would you like to buy our manga?" I thrust a copy in her face, then added, "Half price!" in desperation.

The girl said nothing. She was very strange-looking: blond frizzy hair, oversized dark glasses, and a heavy black sweater that must have been nearly unbearable in the heat.

She slowly extended one arm toward me and put a tiny folded piece of paper into my hand. "Read it," she said, her voice deep and sort of French-sounding.

Elizabeth politely turned away, sensing that the girl didn't want the note read by anyone but me.

I unfolded the piece of paper. It read:

I AM YOU.
FOLLOW ME.

Now, normally when a frizzy-haired, French-sounding blond girl hands you a note that says, "I am you. Follow me," the most prudent course of action is probably to get up and run for the hills. In my case, though, the note caused me only to take a second long look at the girl before me.

About my height. About my build.

If Elizabeth had been looking at my face just then—and she may well have been—she'd have seen a hint of a smile.

It's her.

"Look, um . . . ," I said, turning to a very confused Elizabeth, ". . . this is an old friend of mine." I paused,

realizing it was only proper that I introduce my "old friend" by name. "Her name is . . ." I scoured my brain for a good name—Emily or Katelyn would have done the job—but in my nervousness ended up saying something that was a combination of several names (or perhaps something I'd eaten in an Indian restaurant). ". . . Nata . . . lauri . . . anna."

"Natalaurianna?" repeated Elizabeth, in an astonishing display of listen-and-repeat skills.

"Yeah." My mouth assumed the shape of something that probably didn't look very much like a smile. "Natalaurianna. Very common name . . . where she comes from."

"Nice to meet you, Natalaurianna," said Elizabeth, shooting me a suspicious glance. "So you're from another country?"

I stood up abruptly, terrified at the prospect of what I might come up with for a country name. "Look, Elizabeth, um . . ." I gestured frantically. "Natalaurianna has something she wants to talk to me about. You know, in private."

"Sure," said Elizabeth as I rounded the table. "Take your time."

A minute later the mysterious girl and I were out in the convention center parking lot. I led her to a spot between two enormous minivans and then— making sure no one could see us—asked her to take off the wig and the dark glasses. She obliged, and just as I suspected, I was looking at none other than the Akiko replacement robot: an absolutely identical copy of me that no one—not even my parents—could distinguish from the genuine article.

"You know, a heavy black sweater is maybe not the best disguise choice in the middle of August."

"I'm sorry, Akiko," said the robot, now sounding as much like me as she looked. "I thought it would look suspicious if we were wearing the exact same outfit." Which we soon were, once the robot had removed her sweater and baggy corduroy pants to reveal a T-shirt and khaki shorts just like the ones I was wearing.

I had to smile. The arrival of the Akiko replacement robot in Middleton could only mean one thing: a trip to the planet Smoo. It had been almost a year since my last visit, and I was eager to get back and see my friends. Sure, going to the planet Smoo generally ended up putting me into situations of almost unimaginable danger. Weird thing, I was starting to get *used* to all that danger. Life seemed kind of blah without it.

"So what's going on?" I asked. "Some kind of intergalactic emergency?"

"Not really." The robot smiled. "I was sent here so that you could attend the festivities of Smoovian Liberation Day." She reached into her pocket, produced a small golden lapel-pin kind of thing, and attached it to my shirt.

"Smoovian Liberation Day?" I asked.

"Tomorrow the good people of Smoo will celebrate their one hundred twenty-fifth year of freedom from the tyrannical despot Vorsto Sloggs."

I examined the pin. It was stamped with the smiling face of King Froptoppit and had 125 YEARS engraved along the upper edge. Or rather, it had 100 YEARS engraved, with the 00 scratched out and 25 crudely carved in on top of it.

"They decided to reuse the pins from the one-hundred-year anniversary," explained the robot. "A cost-saving measure."

"So who was Vorsto Sloggs?" I asked. "And how did they finally get rid of him?"

The Akiko robot looked skyward. "I'm sure Mr. Beeba will explain everything to you once you're on board."

"I'm sure he will," I said, rolling my eyes as I imagined Mr. Beeba lecturing me on the details of Smoovian liberation from one end of the universe to the other. "You said 'on board.' So where's the ship?"

The Akiko robot was still looking up into the sky. "See that dot up there?"

I craned my neck. Directly above, so tiny and distant as to be barely distinguishable, was a minuscule speck.

"*That's* the ship?" I shielded my eyes from the sun and squinted to make sure I didn't lose sight of the dot. "What's it doing up there?"

The Akiko robot smiled patiently. "Getting ready to transmoovulate you."

"Trans*moov*ulate me?"

"Mr. Beeba's made a great many improvements,"

she added. "There should be much less of that *about-to-spontaneously-combust* feeling you had last time."

My heart began to beat faster as I recalled this highly disturbing form of beam-me-up transportation. "No, no, look. You tell Mr. Beeba that there is no way on earth—no *way*—I am going to allow him to—"

"Sorry, Akiko." The Akiko robot was waving goodbye. "The process is already under way." She pointed down at my feet—or rather, at the spot where my feet used to be. I felt as if my feet were firmly on the ground, but everything below my ankles had vanished.

The Akiko robot kneeled down and ran her hand through the air between my shins and the ground. "Throwing the transmoovulator into reverse at this stage could result in rearranged internal organs."

I opened my mouth but—in a sudden burst of fondness for my internal organs—found myself unable to raise any further objections. I stared helplessly down at my legs as they gradually vanished below the knee.

"Oh, almost forgot." The Akiko robot dug into her pockets and produced two small pieces of plastic, which she proceeded to jam into my ears. "Brain preservers."

(I tried not think too much about that, or about the fact that I'd gone through transmoovulation once before with nary a brain preserver in sight.)

There was a warm feeling in my belly as the world began to drain itself of color, and soon a vast sea of white surrounded me. I looked down and saw that my body was gone below the navel, and the rest of me was disappearing fast.

dup

dudda-dup

dudda-dup-dup-dup!

The popping noise in my head was considerably quieter than last time. Still, the sea of white glowed brighter and brighter, just as it had before, and just when I thought my eyes were going to be blasted right out from under my eyelids . . .

FFLAAAAAAAAAM!

There was a deafening slamming sound, like a clap of thunder right behind my head. I braced myself, since I recalled that this one would soon be followed by—

FLA-FFLLLAAAAAAAAAAAAAAMMMMMMM!

—another one. Then:

Total silence, apart from the low, steady hum of a powerful engine idling.

I opened my eyes.

I was standing in the middle of a small white room, the main compartment of the spaceship I'd seen as a speck just seconds earlier. I stood perfectly still for a moment, then—fairly certain that my internal organs were still where they were supposed to be—turned full circle in search of my friends: Spuckler, Poog, Gax, and Mr. Beeba. But they were nowhere in sight.

I stepped off the large gray square of the transmoovulator platform and inspected my surroundings. At the front of the ship was a large driver's seat and a bank of controls, with a wide windshield before it and a sea of stars beyond. As far as I could see, there was no one sitting in the driver's seat. The walls were covered with storage compartments and small portals for viewing the passing starscape. And behind me, at the back of the compartment, was a wall occupied by a large rear window and several seats for passengers. But there *were* no passengers.

Or rather, there was only one.

Me.

"Welcome aboard, Akiko."

Chapter 2

It was the voice of Mr. Beeba. But Mr. Beeba was nowhere in sight.

"Um . . ." I walked to the front of the ship, where I thought I'd heard the voice coming from. ". . . where are you?"

"Me?" said the voice of Mr. Beeba, as if I might possibly have been talking to someone else. "Why, I'm back on the planet Smoo, my dear. Marvelous, isn't it?"

As I came around the side of the driver's seat, I saw that there was indeed someone—or something— seated in it: a small legless robot about three feet tall. Its head was like a small portable television attached to the top of a neck. The TV-head pivoted to face me, and there on its grainy five-by-seven-inch screen was the grinning face of Mr. Beeba, eyes sparkling behind his spectacles, waving excitedly with one of his yellow-gloved hands.

"Akiko, meet the Beeba Bot."

I caught my breath for a moment.

They're all still on Smoo. They've sent a robotic chauffeur to pick me up!

"My apologies for not being there in person." The video-screen Mr. Beeba didn't sound particularly apologetic. "But with King Froptoppit having put Spuckler, Gax, Poog, and me in charge of arranging the Smoovian Liberation Day parade, there was simply no time for us to make the trip in person."

I leaned closer to the Beeba Bot's video-screen head, placing my face neatly in front of the tiny camera that was presumably filming me, and said: "Smoovian Liberation Day takes place on the same day every year, right?"

Mr. Beeba looked a little confused. "But of course."

"So you knew it was coming up."

Mr. Beeba now looked uncomfortably sure of

where I was going with this line of questioning. "Certainly."

"So there was plenty of time for you to, oh, I don't know, *send me a letter . . .*" I moved even closer to the camera lens. ". . . *warning* me . . ." I bared my teeth. ". . . that the *Akiko replacement robot* was going to come along and *take me somewhere* to be *transmoovulated* up into a spaceship *with* or *without* my *permission*!"

Mr. Beeba lowered his eyes. "Reprimand received." He fumbled with his fingers. "Loud and clear."

I took a deep breath and briefly considered taking Mr. Beeba further to task. But hey, after my Smoovian friends had paid me a half-dozen such visits—most of them unannounced and some of them much more hair-raising than this one had been so far—it wasn't as though Mr. Beeba's lack of foresight came as any surprise. Besides, I'd been looking forward to this type of craziness for quite some time now, so who was I to complain?

I unfolded a seat from the wall near the front of the ship, sat down, and checked out the view of Earth receding through the window in the back wall. As we sped farther and farther into space, Mr. Beeba told me all about the history of Smoovian Liberation Day. And though I'd expected a long, dry lecture, it turned out to be a rather thrilling tale.

"So let me get this straight," I said after Mr. Beeba had concluded. "This Vorsto Sloggs guy was a horrible dictator whose family ruled the planet Smoo for years and years before King Froptoppit's great-grandfather came along."

"King Froptoppit's great-great-*great*-grandfather," said Mr. Beeba. "Froptoppit the First. He was the daring soul who led the rebellion against the Sloggs family, ending their villainy and starting the infinitely more enlightened rule of the Froptoppits."

"Wow." King Froptoppit had always struck me as a bit of a, well, goofball. It was hard to believe he had descended from a revolutionary hero. "So Froptoppit the First went head to head with Sloggs and beat him, eh?"

"Yes. And the good people of Smoo have lived in freedom ever since."

"Whatever happened to the rest of the Sloggs family?"

"They went into hiding." Mr. Beeba's face took on a look of grave seriousness. "Even today hundreds of Slogg's descendants live secretly among us here on Smoo, and we must remain vigilant to guard against their attempting a return to power. Why, there was a very close call twenty-five years ago, on the very eve of the One Hundredth Liberation Day parade, when a young thief attempted to steal the Misp."

"The Misp?"

"Oh, right," said Mr. Beeba. "I didn't mention that, did I? Vorsto Sloggs derived his powers from a mystical crown that he kept upon his head at all times. It gave him nearly unlimited powers to destroy his enemies. When Froptoppit the First did battle with Vorsto Sloggs that misty morning long ago on Kradpaster Shelf, he was able to knock the crown from Sloggs's head, shattering it to pieces. Only one large piece was left: an indestructible shard called the Misp. Froptoppit the First took the Misp into his possession, and it has remained under close guard ever since."

"I don't get it. It's just a piece of a broken crown. What would anyone want with it?"

Mr. Beeba's video-screen face grew at once more troubled and more animated. "It was the Misp that contained all the crown's powers. A reconstituted crown with the Misp in place could transfer all of Vorsto Sloggs's powers to one of his descendants. Since the Misp cannot be destroyed, the Froptoppits chose long ago to keep it in the palace under their own watchful eyes."

"Wow, so someone tried to steal the thing?"

"Yes, yes." Mr. Beeba's eyes took on the glaze of nostalgia. "Exactly twenty-five years ago, to the day. It was Froptoppit the Fifth himself—or, as you know him, the current King Froptoppit—who caught the would-be thief. His Highness was out for his evening stroll when he caught the little devil trying to scale one of the palace towers."

I was about to ask another question when I noticed that the ship was beginning to turn sideways a bit.

"My apologies, Akiko." Mr. Beeba squinted at me and pushed a button that caused the Beeba Bot to bow its head politely. "That's just the gravitational pull of Pluto. Nothing to be concerned about."

The ship tipped farther to one side as I watched the surface of Pluto zoom past at a proximity that was entirely too close for comfort. As unpredictable as things were when Spuckler was at the wheel, I was pretty sure he'd never almost hit Pluto on the way out of our solar system.

"Mr. Beeba, you *tested* this robot a lot before sending it out to pick me up, right?"

"But of course, Akiko. I put the Beeba Bot through an extremely grueling examination before allowing it to step behind the controls of this ship. Rest assured, the little chap passed with flying colors." Mr. Beeba's video face beamed with pride. "I'll have you know it scored a one hundred percent on the true and false questions and acquitted itself very nearly as well with the fill-in-the-blanks. Why, even its answers for the essay questions were quite good, though understandably somewhat lacking in terms of creative flair."

I blinked at the video screen and tried to stay calm.

"You know, Mr. Beeba, a *written* test is not exactly what I was talking about."

Mr. Beeba's eyes widened momentarily in understanding, then slowly closed under a reassuring brow. "Not to worry, Akiko. The written section was only the first half the test. The second half was entirely oral."

I coughed and leaned forward. *"Oral?"* Staying calm was becoming more of a challenge. "You mean this robot's never been tested in the real world? You let it get behind the wheel of an intergalactic spaceship after nothing more than a *classroom quiz?*"

"An *exam,* Akiko," said Mr. Beeba. "Give me some credit, here, please."

I shook my head and let out a big sigh (big enough, I hoped, for the Beeba Bot's microphone to pick up loud and clear). The sad truth was that, knowing Mr. Beeba as well as I did, this kind of thing was just par for the course.

"Just tell me you didn't devote most of the test to the early history of space travel or changing fashions in tail fin design."

Mr. Beeba remained silent. I tried not to interpret this as a sign that I'd pretty much hit the nail on the head.

"Look, Akiko, everything will be fine. The path

between Earth and Smoo is tried and true. We've flown it so many times now it's as routine as zipping off to the corner store for a gallon of Mubla Milk." Mr. Beeba wobbled his head, then added: "Not that I'm a big fan of Mubla Milk. It doesn't agree with my stomach, to be quite honest."

I took another long look at the stars and decided not to pursue the subject any further. If the Beeba Bot proved to be an unreliable pilot, I told myself, I could always get behind the controls myself. I hadn't tried flying a spaceship since I'd taken Spuckler's place in the Alpha Centauri 5000, but I figured I still remembered enough to scrape by in a pinch.

"Get some sleep, my dear girl, why don't you?" Mr. Beeba's face was supremely calm and confident. "The Beeba Bot and I have everything under control. A bit of rest will do you a world of good."

I moved to the back of the ship, strapped myself into one of the seats, and tried to get some sleep. Judging from my previous trips to Smoo, I still had a long way to go, and I was pretty beat from having woken up so early that morning to staple together a last few issues of *Buckler Spoach*. Slumping down in my seat, I nodded off in a matter of minutes.

Chapter 3

BANG! FLAM! SPRUT—SPRUT—SPRUT—SPRUT!

My eyes flew open. I was upside down. Then right side up. Then upside down again. The Beeba Bot was still at the controls, but it was now jabbing agitatedly at buttons all over the dashboard.

My first thought was that we'd hit an asteroid belt. But beyond the ship's windows was nothing but the same sea of stars I'd always seen on my way to Smoo. Whatever was wreaking havoc with the ship's ability to fly straight, it wasn't asteroids.

"This," I said to myself, "was not on the Beeba Bot's test."

Against my own better judgment, I undid my seat belt and scrambled toward the front of the ship. Compartments within the ship had come open, and their contents were now clattering across the floor in all directions. During the ten seconds it took me to get from one end of the ship to the other, I got struck twice in the head, once in the elbow, and several times in each shin with a variety of airborne objects, some round, some square, all hard as steel and seemingly designed to leave nice big bruises.

When I reached the front of the ship, I grabbed hold of the Beeba Bot's head and turned it around to face me. There, even grainier than before, was the face of Mr. Beeba. His eyes were darting in many directions as he consulted several different books at once.

"Mr. Beeba!" I shouted into the Beeba Bot microphone, instantly gaining Mr. Beeba's wide-eyed attention. "What the heck's going on here?"

"Yes," Mr. Beeba said, as if it were an answer to my question. "Absolutely. I quite understand your concerns, Akiko. I'm, I'm, I'm . . . sure I would be asking the very same question, *verbatim,* were I in your position." He blinked and added, "With the possible exception of the word *heck.*"

"Yeah, well, since you're *not* in my position"—a hard object smacked me in the side of the head and ricocheted off into the windshield—"how about telling me what's freaking this spaceship out?"

"I wish I could say for sure, Akiko." Mr. Beeba turned his eyes back to one of the books before him and adjusted his spectacles. "My working hypothesis at the moment is that you have strayed into an electromagnetic holofield of some sort or another."

"*Holo*field?"

"Fascinating phenomenon, Akiko." Mr. Beeba turned back several pages in search of an earlier passage. "Crops up only once in a millennium. Shame your ship's not equipped with the proper instruments for studying it."

"*Studying* it?" I ducked, dodging by a fraction of an inch a toolbox the size of a microwave oven. It slammed into the dashboard, obliterating a whole panel of buttons and switches. "How about *surviving* it? This ship's getting torn to pieces!"

"Please do try to remain calm, Akiko. I've ordered the Beeba Bot to activate the ship's self-transmoovulation pistons, so that we might—" The video screen went black for a good half minute, then crackled back to life. Mr. Beeba, grainier than ever, was trying very hard to look relaxed and confident. "—and once the ship has rematerialized twenty-five light-years behind your current position, there should be no trouble at all charting a different course. To be sure, it is a bit of a gamble, since I've never actually *tried* transmoovulating an entire ship befo—"

The video screen went black again, this time for much longer.

When it finally came back on, Mr. Beeba was saying: ". . . day you'll look back on all this and wonder why you got yourself so worked up over it."

Just then the Beeba Bot stopped pushing buttons and its arms dropped to its sides. Apart from its video-screen head, it was no longer functioning.

"Best thing you can do right now," continued Mr. Beeba, his voice and face dissolving into static, "is get back to your seat and leave everything to—"

FLAM! FLA-FLAAAAM!

There's no other way to describe it: the Beeba Bot's head exploded. I turned my face just in time to avoid fiery shards flying into my eyes. When I turned back, there was nothing left of the Beeba Bot but the charred and smoking lower half of its body.

No one's piloting the ship!

I grabbed what was left of the Beeba Bot, unstrapped it from the driver's seat, and tossed it aside. But before I could take its place and begin to make sense of how to steer the ship . . .

THWOK!

Pain! Stabbing, burning pain as something hard and heavy hit me squarely in the back of the head.

I saw the dashboard and the stars beyond dissolve into a blur of double vision. Then everything went black.

Chapter 4

When I opened my eyes, the interior of the ship was dark, silent, and utterly still. I lay there motionless for a minute or two, slowly piecing together where I was and—to whatever extent I could— what had just happened.

After I'd made sure that all my limbs still worked and that I wasn't bleeding anywhere (or not bleeding very *much,* anyway), I dug myself out of the assorted spaceship junk I was half buried beneath and found the emergency exit in the ship's ceiling. By twisting a handle in the center of the door and pulling on it with all my might . . .

K'CHAK

. . . I was able to push the hatch open. Bright white light poured in, blinding me for a moment, while dust and hot air blasted me in the face.

Smoo, I thought. *I'm on Smoo. I can* smell *it.*

And I could, too. I'd never really noticed it until then, but Smoo had a smell all its own—just the tiniest trace of something floral and sweet in the air— and without trying to, I had memorized that smell over time. I took another deep whiff.

Yep, that's Smoo. No mistaking it.

I ran a hand through my hair, removing a couple of pieces of spaceship debris in the process.

All right. I'm still alive and I know where I am. Two things to be grateful for.

And, yes, there were a great many things I *wasn't* particularly grateful for. But intergalactic travel has a way of teaching you to focus on the positive.

I took a deep breath, placed my hands on either side of the exit portal, and pulled myself out into the open air.

It was midday. The Smoovian sun was directly

above in the middle of a cloudless sky. It quickly warmed my arms and shoulders and the top of my head.

I rose to my feet and inspected the spaceship. The little of it I could *see,* anyway: it had cut a mile-long trench in the ground and nearly burrowed completely underground by the time it came to a stop. Its wings and tail fins were battered and scarred. A large section of its hull was peeled back like the lid of a sardine can.

I turned my eyes to the horizon, hoping to find something—anything—familiar. Smoo was an awfully big planet, and I knew from hard experience how many days it could take to get from one part of

it to another on foot. From where I stood, though, I could see nothing but treeless hills and craggy white mountains in all directions. I had clearly landed in the middle of an uninhabited desert.

Still, it looked a little familiar. The rock formations and the color of the sand bore a striking resemblance to the land near King Froptoppit's palace. It looked a little wilder, less tame somehow, but with any luck the palace wasn't far off. Maybe the ship's homing device was one of the few things that had still been working before the crash. Maybe, just maybe, it had gotten me within a few miles of where I needed to be.

"All right, Mr. Beeba," I said with a smile. "You may be out of the doghouse after all."

I climbed back into the ship and dug around for provisions. I managed to find a canteen of water and a tin full of chalky biscuitlike things. I tucked one of them under each arm and set off in search of someone who might save me from wasting away in the Smoovian desert.

The rest of the afternoon was spent trekking across huge expanses of sand and rock, occasionally climbing to the tops of hills in hopes of seeing the palace somewhere on the horizon. The hours passed. The sun sank perilously low in the sky. Then, just as I reached the summit of a steep rocky hill, I saw it: King Froptoppit's palace. Its central tower rose majestically above the plain in the distance, creating a pale purplish silhouette that at that particular moment seemed to be the most beautiful thing I'd ever seen.

"King Froptoppit!" I bellowed, fully aware that neither the king nor anyone else would hear. "Don't lock the gates! I'm on my way!"

Talk about getting a second wind: I was so pumped full of adrenaline I practically sprinted the last three miles to the palace without even having to catch my breath. I sang and whistled and laughed out loud like a crazy person. I was saved. Everything was going to turn out just fine.

But as I ran, a very strange thing happened. The

closer I got to King Froptoppit's palace, the more I began to see that it was *not* King Froptoppit's palace.

I mean, it *was* his palace.

It just wasn't *all* of his palace.

It was smaller. A lot smaller. It was as if he'd decided to take the outer two-thirds of it and tear it all down. And not just that, either. By the time I got within a mile of the palace grounds, I could see that where whole city blocks of towers and rooftops used to be, there was now nothing but hills, trees, and grasslands. It was as if King Froptoppit had decided not only to get rid of the some of the most beautiful parts of his home, but also to painstakingly re-create the landscape that had been there before the buildings were put up.

"This is weird," I said to myself, slowing to a trot.

I thought for a moment about what I'd just said.

"Even weirder than usual."

Chapter 5

"Who goes there?"

I was standing at the palace gates, gazing up at a pair of Smoovian sentries in a guard tower. I recognized them from the big party King Froptoppit had thrown for me and Spuckler and everybody after we'd rescued the Prince from the castle of Alia Rellapor. I'd stood and talked to them for a good half hour while they served everyone smagberry punch. It took me a few seconds of racking my brain, but I finally remembered their names.

"Kooch! McBarp!" Their eyes widened, but only in shock, not recognition. "It's me! Akiko!"

Kooch, the taller of the two, leaned over the

guardrail at the top of the tower and squinted at me. Something was different about him, but I couldn't put my finger on it.

"How do you know our names?"

Then it hit me. I'd grown a lot since the time of the party. I was in the sixth grade now, not the fourth. Of course they'd have trouble recognizing me.

"The party," I said. "Remember? After I led the mission to rescue Prince Froptoppit. You guys were serving punch." Thinking it might trigger memories, I added: "Remember when Spuckler knocked the punch bowl over and it landed right on top of Gax? Poor robot's *still* got smagberries inside him, I bet!"

Kooch and McBarp gave each other a strange look: a look that I knew all too well from kids at school. It was a classic *we're-dealing-with-someone-who's-got-a-few-screws-loose-so-be-careful-what-you-say-because-it-doesn't-take-much-to-make-people-like-this-totally-wig-out* look.

McBarp—who appeared to have lost a bit of weight since I last saw him—elbowed Kooch aside and adopted the overly gentle voice of a grown-up explaining things to a toddler.

"Look, sweetheart, why don't you go on home. I'm sure you mean no harm, but making up stories to try to get past the palace gates is pretty serious business."

Now it was my turn to look shocked. How could they not remember me? Especially after the punch bowl story.

Stay calm. There's a nice hot meal waiting for you if you can get past these guys.

I took a deep breath.

"All right, all right." I waved my hands in the air, as if to erase the last few minutes of conversation and get a fresh start. "You don't remember me. Not a big deal: it's been a couple of years. I'm sure you meet lots of people in your line of work, and you can't be expected to remember everybody." I tried to refrain from being sarcastic but couldn't resist: "Especially, you know, insignificant people who *risked life and limb to rescue the Prince of Smoo.*"

Kooch and McBarp gave each other pretty much the same look they'd exchanged a moment earlier. Only more so.

"So just go tell Mr. Beeba I'm here and he'll clear everything up."

This time their surprise was tinged with a bit of respect.

Kooch narrowed his eyes. "You . . . know Mr. Beeba?"

All right, now we're getting somewhere.

"Know him? *Know* him?" It was hard to keep from laughing. "Well, let's see. I've only gone to half a dozen different *planets* with the guy, saved him from getting thrown into boiling hot lava at the top of Mount Vorf—excuse me, *Volcano* Vorf—and sat right next to him while we both got covered from head to toe with Almost-Black-Hole mucus." I paused to let all that sink in. "Yeah. I think you could say I know Mr. Beeba." I folded my arms and delivered the final blow: "Better than *you two* know him, I'll bet."

McBarp blinked several times and took a deep breath. Then he said to Kooch, without taking his eyes from mine, "Go get Mr. Beeba."

Chapter 6

Just under five minutes later Kooch returned with Mr. Beeba. They came from around the corner of a vine-covered tower that was some distance from me, and from where I was standing it looked like Mr. Beeba was wearing . . . well, there's no other way of putting it: a bad wig.

Where normally the top of his head was smooth and hairless, it now sported an impressive pompadour, one that stood several inches above him in a way that—if not quite defying gravity—was certainly trying to show gravity who was boss. He was also much, much thinner than he'd been the last time I'd seen him (which had been just a few hours earlier, by way of the Beeba Bot's video screen). It all added up to one thing: Mr. Beeba had become younger. A *lot* younger. He had somehow reversed the aging process and subtracted a good twenty or thirty years from his appearance.

Only then did it occur to me that the same could be said of Kooch and McBarp. I was less familiar with their faces, so it hadn't hit me before. But they looked younger in much the same way Mr. Beeba did.

The palace. The palace is smaller than the last time I saw it.

Mr. Beeba stepped forward and looked at me without the slightest shred of recognition. It was as if he were seeing me for the first time.

No. It's not as if. He is *seeing me for the first time.*

I recalled the words Mr. Beeba had said just before the Beeba Bot's head exploded: "I've ordered the Beeba Bot to activate the ship's self-transmoovulation pistons. . . ."

Mr. Beeba tried to transmoovulate me away from the holofield.

"—and once the ship has rematerialized twenty-five light-years behind your current position, there should be no trouble at all charting a different course."

I looked at Mr. Beeba's chest. Sure enough, he was wearing the same lapel pin I was, but with the 100 YEARS untouched. The pieces slid together in my mind and all at once I understood.

He tried to send me back in space. He ended up sending me back in time!

Mr. Beeba bowed politely and cleared his throat to speak. "The guards inform me that you have attempted to present yourself as an acquaintance of mine." His eyes searched mine, sizing me up. I could almost hear his thoughts: *Is she deliberately deceiving us? Or is she suffering from a delusion and merely deceiving herself?*

Mr. Beeba paused and ran a hand across his carefully tended yellow pompadour. "I expect there is an explanation for your behavior. I will now give you an opportunity to present that explanation, but you should bear two things in mind: First"—he counted then with the fingers of one hand—"be succinct. We are in the midst of preparations for the One Hundredth Liberation Day parade tomorrow, and everyone here at the palace is extremely busy, me foremost among them."

I'm exactly twenty-five years in the past. To the day.

"Second, you should in the process be entirely truthful, as I assure you it would be highly unwise to compound these flagrant fabrications of yours with further falsities." (One thing's for sure: the Mr. Beeba of the past knew just as many big words as the Mr. Beeba of the present.)

I stepped forward to the palace gates, pressed my face between two of the bars, and motioned for Mr. Beeba to come closer. He paused and turned to Kooch and McBarp, confirming that they were ready to step in if I tried any funny business. Then he moved forward until his face was no more than a foot from mine.

I opened my mouth and spoke: "I'm . . ."

I probably should have thought about what I was going to say before I motioned Mr. Beeba over.

"I'm . . ."

It would have been the smart thing to do.

"I'm . . ."

Still, all the thought in the world wouldn't have made what I needed to say sound any less ridiculous.

"I'm . . ."

Mr. Beeba moved his face several inches forward and allowed his eyelids to slide down more than halfway over his pupils. "You're what?"

I swallowed, and tensed my face into what I hoped was a highly trustworthy look.

Then I whispered: "I'm from the future."

Mr. Beeba's eyes widened. He took a single step back and blinked once or twice. I tried to read some sort of reaction in his eyes. Did he believe me? Did he think I was nuts? It was hard to tell.

"You're from the future." He said it calmly, as if rolling the explanation around in his mind and trying to get used to it.

I've got him. He's ready to believe me. All I've gotta do is explain a little.

"That's right. The future. You sent me through a time warp. Not the you of right now. The you of the future. You didn't *mean* to. It was an accident. You were trying to transmoovulate me."

Mr. Beeba's eyelids dropped down just a touch.

"Um, and I understand that maybe transmoovulation doesn't even exist yet. And that time travel into the past breaks a lot of the fundamental laws of . . . you know . . ." The word I was searching for was *physics*. ". . . physical education. But this—honestly—is the real explanation for why you think you don't know me. You see, you *do* know me. You just don't *know* that you know me. *Yet*. You're *going* to know that you know me, you know? In the *fu-*ture." My voice cracked a little on the "few" part of *future*. This explaining business was a lot harder than I thought.

Mr. Beeba turned to Kooch and McBarp and without the slightest hesitation said: "Send her to

53

the delusional children's ward. They'll know what to do with her." He ran a gloved hand through his absurdly large pompadour and turned to leave.

"Wait!" I shouted. "I can prove all this." I grabbed hold of my lapel pin and pointed at it with a jittery urgency. "See this pin? It says 'One hundred twenty-five years.' I've come to you from twenty-five years in the future."

Mr. Beeba turned back around to face me. He leaned toward me and examined the pin.

"Your lapel pin is identical to mine. The only difference is that some idiot has scratched out the zeroes and carved a twenty-five in their place."

I sputtered a bit but said nothing. Mr. Beeba was right. The lapel pin only made my story look more like a desperate hoax.

"Okay, forget the pin." I locked my eyes on Mr. Beeba's and spoke as forcefully as I could. "I can tell you about things that happen to you in the future. Things that I couldn't possibly be making up."

Mr. Beeba raised a finger to his chin and took a deep breath. He seemed curious.

"Very well, then." He folded his arms across his chest. "Tell me about . . . the me of the future."

"Okay. So, in the future Prince Froptoppit gets kidnapped." I paused and added: "Is there a Prince Froptoppit yet?"

"No," said Mr. Beeba, "but there will no doubt be one in the years to come, after His Majesty finds a suitable bride."

"All right, so in the future there's a Prince Froptoppit. And he gets kidnapped, and you and I end up being part of the rescue party. I shouldn't say *party,* because it was anything but, if you know what I mean. Incredibly dangerous stuff. Sky pirates. Giant water snakes. The Great Wall of Trudd. We'd have never made it through without Spuckler, Gax, and Poog."

Mr. Beeba rose a finger to stop me. "I do indeed have a dear friend by the name of Poog. He works with me here in the palace. But those other names are entirely unfamiliar to me."

"Okay, but that's only because you haven't met them yet. You will. Trust me."

Mr. Beeba wobbled his head a bit. "Go on."

"Okay, well, that's just one of the adventures we go on. One time you took—er, will take me to the Intergalactic Zoo on the planet Quilk and help rescue me when I get captured and put into a humanoid collection. Then you'll be along when we all try to win the Alpha Centauri 5000. And then you'll take me to Poog's home planet, Toog, to save him when he's in trouble."

Mr. Beeba smiled. "Nice try, my dear. You nearly had me." His face now turned stony and cold. "Any fool could tell you I am a timid academic. The very idea of my consenting to get involved in such madness as rescue missions and intergalactic rocket ship races is preposterous poppycock."

"But it's true! I'm not making this—"

"Begone, my child. Go back to whence you

came, before I have these guards chase you away forcibly." And with that he pivoted on one heel and marched away from me at top speed.

"I can tell you other things! Things that don't sound so crazy!"

Mr. Beeba kept marching away.

"We go to the training camp on Zarga Baffa!"

He was nearing the corner where he'd vanish from view.

"We help put Gax back together! You know, Gax! The robot you're going to meet in the future!"

He chuckled loudly before marching out of sight.

In my desperation I decided to shout the only thing I could think of that would get him to stop.

"You're put in charge of all the libraries in the entire galaxy!"

Dead silence.

Then, ever so slowly, Mr. Beeba's pompadoured head peeped around the corner.

"What was that?"

I swallowed hard and—promising myself that I'd tell him the truth later—added a few more lies to the first one.

"To, um, save the libraries from, uh . . . poor management, they make all of the galaxy's librarians answer directly to you."

Mr. Beeba could not disguise his pleasure at hearing this.

"Emperor of libraries," I added. "That's your, uh, official title."

Mr. Beeba smiled and began to walk back toward me.

"Emperor of libraries. *Really*."

"Yeah. It's, uh, like a dream come true for you. I mean, no adventures. Nothing dangerous. Just books, books, books. All day long. For the rest of your life."

Mr. Beeba was now standing in front of me again, stroking his chin approvingly. "Yes, well, *that's* sounding much more plausible."

I leaned forward. "Let me in," I whispered, "and I'll tell how you get voted Most Brilliant Guy Ever."

Mr. Beeba blinked. "*Guy?* Do they really use the word *guy?*"

"*Man* Ever. Most Brilliant *Man* Ever."

There was a long pause as Mr. Beeba considered this new information—or *mis*information, I should say—and factored it into his decision-making process. He turned to the guards and spoke with authority.

"Let her in. It seems she's telling the truth after all."

Chapter 7

Boy, did things improve after that. Once Mr. Beeba became convinced that I was a visitor from his own gloriously book-filled future, he began treating me so much like an old friend it was almost as if he *did* remember me. First thing he did was take me to his study, where we were soon visited by Poog.

As soon as I saw him I ran over to get as close as I could without, you know, hugging him and freaking him out. Like Mr. Beeba, Poog looked much younger. His eyes were larger in proportion to his face, and his skin was a darker shade of purple.

Mr. Beeba stood at my side and gestured, much

as he would years later in similar situations. "Allow me to introduce you—or *re*introduce you, as the case may be—to Poog."

"Nice to meet you, Poog," I said. "I'm Akiko."

Poog blurted out something in his warbly, gurgly language.

Mr. Beeba translated: "Poog says he has heard of time travelers before but has never encountered one face to face. He is honored to make your acquaintance."

Just then I noticed a framed picture on the wall, one that I was very sure Mr. Beeba no longer had hanging there when I met him twenty-five years in the future. It was an image of a very tall man with a gaunt face and frizzy white hair.

"Mr. Beeba, who is this a picture of?"

Mr. Beeba narrowed his eyes a bit. "Now, hold on a moment. If you're from the future, surely you know him. I'm sure I would have spoken with you about him on a great number of occasions."

"But you haven't," I said. "I mean, you won't. In

the future you no longer have this picture hanging here."

"Hmm." Mr. Beeba stroked his chin. "I can't imagine taking this picture down. It is a picture of my mentor, Professor Norkenhoozen. A wise and brilliant man of science I am exceedingly proud to count among my personal friends. He is, among many other things, one of the planet Smoo's foremost experts on the legendary crown of Grazz G'bah."

"Well, you may be in for some selective memory loss in the future, Mr. Beeba, because I'm very sure you never end up mentioning the name Norkenhoozen to me." I gave Mr. Beeba a knowing look. "I mean, come on. I wouldn't forget a name like that."

"No," Mr. Beeba said as he regarded the picture thoughtfully. "No, I don't suppose you would."

From there the conversation turned to books, science, and, not surprisingly, Mr. Beeba's future exploits as emperor of libraries. Then Mr. Beeba abruptly clapped his hands together and began to march from the room.

"Come," he said. "We must introduce you to the king. He will be very interested to hear how his reign will proceed in the years to come."

And so we went off to the king's chambers. With Mr. Beeba vouching for me, no one had any doubts about the validity of my story. It was decided, in fact, that I should not only meet the king but also be his guest for dinner. And so it was that I soon found myself seated at a food-laden table in a cavernous dining hall, with Mr. Beeba on my right and Poog on my left, all three of us waiting anxiously for the arrival of King Froptoppit.

"This is quite an honor," Mr. Beeba whispered to me. "Normally King Froptoppit dines alone, and at a much later hour. Why, he even canceled his evening stroll for this."

Something about that last sentence snagged my attention.

Evening stroll. Mr. Beeba said something earlier about King Froptoppit's evening stroll. What was it?

Before I could devote more thought to the question, there was a mighty blaring of trumpets and King Froptoppit entered the room.

This King Froptoppit was a rather more dashing figure than the one I knew. His hair had not yet gone white—it was still jet black in places—and his mustache was much more neatly trimmed. He was thinner, though he already had a touch of the potbelly he would later develop, and his movements were more lively and energetic. This was King Froptoppit in his prime.

"A pleasure to make your acquaintance, my dear girl," he said, grinning from ear to ear as he stepped to my side and gave my hand a vigorous shaking. "I am Froptoppit, king of Smoo."

"I'm Akiko," I said, smiling. "Sixth grader."

"What are you waiting for? Dig in!" He winked, then added: "But save room for dessert! Smagberry upside-down-and-inside-out cake. I've got the royal chefs making an extralarge one just for this occasion."

And so the four of us shared an incredible meal, every bit as delicious as anything I'd have years later. I entertained the king with stories of the future, drawing gasps and chuckles by turn as I revealed each new piece of information. I had very nearly reached the end of my recounting of the showdown with Throck when . . .

"Sire! Sire!" One of King Froptoppit's servants came dashing into the room, out of breath and red-faced. "A thief! One of the palace guards has apprehended a thief attempting to steal the Misp!"

Chapter 8

The meal was abandoned and we all ran off through the palace to see the would-be Misp thief. By now I had recalled Mr. Beeba's earlier mention of King Froptoppit's evening stroll and its significance: "It was Froptoppit the Fifth himself—or, as you know him, the current King Froptoppit—who caught the would-be thief. His Highness was out for his evening stroll when he caught the little devil trying to scale one of the palace towers."

Wow. So my arrival here has altered the course of Smoovian history. Instead of King Froptoppit catching the thief, one of the guards ended up catching him.

I found this a little troubling. Altering the course

of history was pretty serious business. But at least the thief had still gotten caught. Did it really matter who caught him?

We ran through one final corridor and arrived in the storage chamber. On the far end of the room was a wall safe. It had evidently already been broken into, for its massive door was wide open. It was illuminated from within, showing that it was completely empty.

In the middle of the room was an incredibly heavyset guard, sitting on the chest of the would-be thief, a small man with close-cropped hair. The thief's face was turned away from me, and his lower body was entirely obscured by the massive torso of the guard.

"Here it is, sire," said the guard, proudly displaying a small orange-colored object that looked like a shard of an ancient vase. "The Misp. Caught him red-handed trying to make off with it."

I took a few steps closer to get a better view of the thief, who wore a bright red suit. He had spiky

black hair and—I very nearly smacked my forehead when I saw it—a peg leg.

Oh, please.

He was relatively young—little more than a teenager—and lacked the customarily heavy five o'clock shadow of his adulthood. The best he could do for now was a very small patch of stubble on his chin that made him look like a hipster at a coffee shop.

"Dagnabbit, get yer fat bee-hind offa me!" he cried in his high-pitched teenager's voice, unable to move beneath the weight of the huge guard. "Ya got me cuffed an' shackled. I ain't goin' nowhere. And where's my Gax unit? Whadja do with him?"

The guard chuckled and said nothing, grinning like a fisherman who'd just netted the biggest catch of his life.

"Well done, Fatch," said King Froptoppit, stepping forward to inspect the young man he did not yet know as Spuckler Boach. "Let's get that Misp back where it belongs."

King Froptoppit took the Misp from Fatch and carefully replaced it in the wall safe. "The whole of Smoo has been saved this night from a hideous fate. And we owe it all to you, Fatch."

"You honor me, sire," said Fatch. "It was just dumb luck that I was the one who nabbed him. An hour or two later and I'd have been down guarding the transport hangar instead of here."

Mr. Beeba joined King Froptoppit in congratulating Fatch. "I'll see to it that you are generously rewarded for this, my good fellow. *Very* generously. And what's this I hear about a Gax unit?"

"A robot cohort," said Fatch. "Kooch and McBarp found him at the bottom of the tower, waiting in getaway mode. They immobilized him and had him put in your lab for safekeeping."

"Top-notch work," said Mr. Beeba before narrowing his eyes at Spuckler. "We can all sleep soundly tonight, thanks to your having apprehended this young rapscallion."

"I ain't no scallion!" cried Spuckler, trying

unsuccessfully once again to roll out from underneath Fatch.

I moved around Mr. Beeba to get a closer look at young Spuckler.

"There must be some kind of mistake," I said to Mr. Beeba. "This is no thief. This is Spuckler. Spuckler Boach."

Everyone in the room gasped in amazement at my producing this name, no one more loudly than Spuckler himself, who, naturally enough, had no idea who I was or how I had come to know his name.

"You . . ." Mr. Beeba stared at me with cautious eyes. ". . . *know* him?"

"Oh, sure," I said.

"She's lyin'!" protested Spuckler, apparently not the least bit grateful for my having said a few words in his defense. "I ain't never laid eyes on her in my life." He paused and, as if determined to make things worse for himself, continued: "And I am *too* a thief. Thirteen years behind the belt, and proud of it."

"Silence!" said Mr. Beeba. "Another word out of you and I'll have you carted off to the darkest cell in the palace dungeon."

Spuckler moaned but followed orders.

"Very well, then." Mr. Beeba turned to me and squinted with intense curiosity. "Please enlighten us, young lady, as to how it is you became an accomp—" He stopped himself and started again with a different word. "—acquaintance of this young man."

"Well, I first met him when, let's see. . . ." I thought for a moment. It had been so long. "Oh, I remember: I first met Spuckler when you took me out to his ranch and introduced me to him."

Mr. Beeba's eyes bugged out a bit before returning to their normal size. "*I* . . . introduced him to *you?*" He squinted at me with newfound suspicion. "Forgive me for doubting you, my dear, but I do believe it is *you* who just introduced him to *me*." He paused long enough for me to realize there was no way to deny this simple fact. "A few seconds ago."

"Oh, yeah. Well . . ." I smiled and laughed nervously. "You're right about that, aren't you? Yeah, I, uh, knew his name, and, um, you didn't, so—"

Mr. Beeba cut me off, now seemingly no longer on my side. "Explain yourself, child. If you are a friend of this young thief, you must take responsibility for your own poor judgment of character. And I hasten to add that it does you no good to cloud the issue by attempting to pin the whole affair on me."

"Quite right," said King Froptoppit. "An explanation is in order."

There was an uncomfortable silence. All eyes were on me—even Poog was watching me suspiciously—and I was beginning to wonder if I should have kept quiet about knowing Spuckler.

"It's simple." I tried to clear my throat but found my mouth too dry to pull it off. "You *did* introduce me to Spuckler. You just don't remember it because it hasn't happened yet." I winced involuntarily at the sheer insanity of what I'd just said. "But it's *going* to happen, in, in . . . the future."

"Ahhh . . . ," said Mr. Beeba, somehow making the *ahhh* sound like an expression of great doubt. "The future."

"Look, none of that really matters," I said, though I was certain that at the moment there was little that mattered more to Mr. Beeba. "The important thing is that you realize Spuckler is on your side."

"No, I ain't," said Spuckler. "You're all nutcases."

"Silence!" Mr. Beeba extended his index finger until it was only inches from Spuckler's nose. "This is your last chance, boy. I'm warning you!"

After a moment Mr. Beeba turned and locked his eyes on mine, as if to say, "This is *your* last chance too."

I took a deep breath. "Look, it comes down to this: he's a good guy. Or he's *going* to be a good guy. I know it doesn't look that way now, but you've got to trust me on this. I'm from the future, and I know how all of this is going to work out. You and Spuckler are going to be friends. Best *buddies*, even." (Okay, they'd be at each other's throats half the time too, but I had the sense to keep that to myself.)

Mr. Beeba paused for a very long time. He stared at me, and then at Spuckler, and then at me again. When at last he spoke, his voice was cold and unemotional.

"My mentor, Professor Norkenhoozen—whose name and face, interestingly enough, you find entirely unfamiliar—always used to tell me that the simplest explanation is invariably the true one." He began to pace around the room. "There is an exceedingly simple explanation for your knowing this man's name . . ." Mr. Beeba came to a stop and shot me a glance that went straight through me. ". . . and I assure you it has nothing whatsoever to do with people traveling through time." He resumed his pacing. "No, the simplest explanation is this: you are a coconspirator of his."

"A *what*?" I couldn't believe what I was hearing.

"Come now, child. You came to us as a distraction. I can't believe I didn't see it sooner. Your whole reason for being here"—Mr. Beeba pointed his finger at Spuckler—"was to keep us from discovering *him*!"

I opened my mouth but no words came. What could I say? Mr. Beeba's explanation sounded eminently believable, while my explanation—the truth—sounded like a pack of lies.

"That's not true!" I said at last. "You've got to belie—"

"Silence!" cried Mr. Beeba with a sharp wave of his hand, then turned and bowed to King Froptoppit. "With your permission, sire, I will have both of them sent to the palace dungeon while we deliberate upon their fate."

King Froptoppit nodded his agreement. "The dungeon." He turned on his heel and strolled back out of the room. "Perfect place for thieves like these."

Chapter 9

"Ya can't do this t' me!"

Spuckler was screaming in a surprisingly high-pitched voice as the guards carted the two of us off to our cells. "I ain't never been in jail b'fore! I won't last a minute in there!" He sounded like a first grader being taken to the principal's office.

The guards had begun by trying to calm Spuckler down but had finally given up and just started to ignore him.

"Mercy! Have mercy!" Spuckler let out a wail so pathetic you'd have thought he was being dragged before a firing squad. "Merrrrrr-saaaaay!"

Jeez. I had no idea Spuckler used to be such a wimp about this kind of thing.

K'JENK!

One of the guards yanked a rusty cell door open and threw Spuckler in headfirst. There was a thunderous crash as Spuckler somersaulted into the rickety wooden bed in the back of the cell and—from the sound of it—totally demolished it.

"I'm bleedin' in here! Bleeeeeeedin', d'ya hear me?"

The other guard opened a door opposite Spuckler's and pushed me into the cell beyond it.

"Look," I said. "Just tell Mr. Beeba to go over things carefully in his mind. If he thinks all this through, he'll realize that everything I've said—crazy as it sounds—is true."

The guard just laughed, loud and long enough for me to smell his awful breath, and slammed the cell door in my face.

F'CHANK!

The guards whistled as they strolled back down the hall, taking the one good source of light with them.

"Lemme outta here!" Spuckler sounded as if he was bawling his eyes out. "I can't take it! Can't taaaake it!" He continued like that for several minutes, crying out for freedom, forgiveness, his mama, you name it.

Me, I chose to stay quiet and try to assess the situation.

Well, things could be worse. At least I'm not seriously hurt. And there's bound to be some sort of legal procedure that kicks in sooner or later. If I'm able to argue our case before King Froptoppit, maybe—

"Suckers." It was Spuckler. He had stuck a hand out his cell door, with a small mirror in it, expertly tilted to show him the end of the corridor where the guards had exited. "Come on, guys, make it a challenge, at least. Ya ain't got nothing on that hallway door but a dagnabbed single-bind Orpston lock."

He flipped the mirror around with the practiced hand of a cardsharp and checked out the rest of the hallway. "Pick them things in my sleep, for cryin' out loud."

His voice was utterly calm, without even a trace of the pants-wetting panic he'd been in only a

minute earlier. Seeing that I had my eyes on him, he turned and gave me a wink. "You okay?"

I smiled. "Yeah, I'm fine." I paused and gave him a knowing look. "So how is it that a boy who 'ain't never been in jail b'fore' carries a little mirror like that with him?"

Spuckler grinned. "Lady, you're lookin' at a kid who's been in every jail between here and the moons of Jagoozi." (I was about to correct him for calling me "lady," but the truth is we were no longer that far apart in age, and for all I knew he was right to assume I was older than him.) "I'm a safecracker by trade. That's how I got hired for this Misp-stealin' gig. And breakin' into safes and breakin' outta jails are two sides of the same coin, s'far as I'm concerned. Heck, I ain't been in a jail yet that could hold me for more'n half an hour."

He sure did talk the talk. But who was to say it wasn't just a lot of hot air?

"Okay, hotshot," I said, looking at my watch. "I'll give you ten minutes to get us out of this one."

KREEEEEeeeeee

Spuckler's cell door swung open. He jumped to his feet, strolled out into the hallway, and gave his neck a good crack. "Sorry, lady. I must've thought ya said *seconds*."

Chapter 10

No doubt about it: Spuckler, even as a teenager, was every bit the jail-breaking expert he claimed to be. Before I knew it, he had both of us out of the dungeon area and back in the palace proper.

"First thing we gotta do"—Spuckler was holding a wad of papers that looked to be blueprints of the entire palace—"is go find my robot."

"You mean Gax?" I asked.

Spuckler's jaw dropped.

"Oh yeah," I said. "I'm not supposed to know that name yet."

"I ain't gonna ask," said Spuckler, returning his attention to the blueprints. "Looks like the lab'ratory's on the other side of the palace. If we crawl through the air vents, it'll be a pretty straight shot."

So Spuckler popped open a nearby grate and the two of us crawled inside. As we made our way from one narrow passage to the next, I decided it was time to get some more information about how Spuckler had ended up trying to steal the Misp.

"So, Spuckler. You said your safecracking skills are what landed you this job."

"Got that right."

"Okay, then who hired you? Who was it that wanted the Misp so badly?"

Spuckler stopped crawling for a moment and peered back at me. "Well now, I ain't exactly sure. I met the guy in an alley outside a pool hall on the planet Kwamp. It was real dark an' shadowy, and I never did get a good look at his face, on account of he had it wrapped up under bandages. Black bandages." He paused, then added, "Looked kinda cool, actually."

Well, so much for getting a good description.

"How tall was he?"

"Pretty tall. Taller'n me, for sure. And he had a funny walk. Like both his legs were real stiff."

"What did his voice sound like?"

"Well, that was the weirdest thing. He never said a word. Wrote everything down on a pad of paper and made me read it."

I thought this over. "Do you think he was mute, or just choosing not to talk?"

Spuckler considered the possibilities. "Don't rightly know, lady. Don't rightly know." He rubbed his fingers across the patch of whiskers on his chin that would one day grow into a thick stubble. "One thing's for sure. He was goin' outta his way to keep anyone from knowin' much of anything about him. Had plenty of secrets, that feller, you can bank on it."

A descendant of that tyrant guy, Sloggs, I thought. *It's got to be. But which one? Mr. Beeba said there were hundreds of them on Smoo, all of them very careful to keep their identities concealed.*

"All right, lady, this is it." Spuckler turned back and gave me a thumbs-up. "The lab's on the other side of this here vent."

All right. If we can grab Gax and get out of here, I can at least live the rest of my life outside of a dungeon.

Spuckler began to pry open the vent, but I stopped him.

"One thing."

"What's that?"

"You've got to stop calling me 'lady.'" I smiled. "I may not have been your accomplice before, but I sure am now. My name's Akiko."

"'Kiko," said Spuckler. "Real pleased to meetcha."

Spuckler finished prying the vent open, and we crawled out onto the clean, porcelain-like floor beyond. There were dozens of tables, each piled high with test tubes, beakers, and strange machines and instruments whose purposes I'd never be able to guess in million years.

At the far end of the room, inside a large glass

box, was Gax. Not, of course, the Gax I knew: that Gax was only to emerge after twenty more years of accumulated grime, dents, and assorted wear and tear (most of it entirely unnecessary, no doubt), courtesy of Spuckler Boach. The Gax before me now was a cleaner, shinier Gax, a Gax that looked as if it had rolled off the factory floor just a few months earlier. The other key difference was that he was as still as a statue at the moment. Maybe someone had somehow switched him off.

"Purty slick, ain't he?" Spuckler stepped forward and let loose an admiring whistle, like a boy checking out a brand-new Corvette. "You got no idea how long it took me to save enough gilpots for this little fella."

Spuckler opened the glass door, pulled Gax out, and carefully placed him on the laboratory floor. "What's this they stuck on ya here? An immobilizer patch?" He squinted with displeasure at a metallic device about the size of a matchbox that had been affixed to Gax's body. "Don't they know these things leave a mark? Now, that's just rude, is what that is."

"I can't believe how clean he still is," I said, circling Gax as Spuckler worked to remove the device. "I'll bet you haven't gone on many adventures with him yet, have you?"

"Adventures?" Spuckler looked up at me long enough to chuckle and roll his eyes. "Lady, me and Gax are thieves. We don't *do* adventures."

I smiled. "Well, you better get used to the idea, Spucky. Because I have a feeling you two'll be getting into a different line of work one of these days."

K'CHUK!

The door to the lab! Someone was coming in!

Chapter 11

It didn't take very long to evaluate our options: we basically didn't have any.

Well, unless you call sitting there slack-jawed while someone strolled in and caught us trying to steal the robot an option.

The funny thing is, it took the person—Mr. Beeba's lab assistant—an awfully long time to see us there. By the looks of her Coke-bottle glasses, she didn't have terribly good eyesight. In fact, it didn't look as if she had terribly good *anything*. She was short and hunched over, like a grandmother with a very bad back, and had a bizarrely large beehive hairdo that towered so high above her head it nearly doubled her height.

She actually did a mini tour of the whole lab—sniffing petri dishes and watering plants, checking charts and dusting off bookshelves—before coming anywhere near us. She pottered around like that for a good five minutes while Spuckler and I stared at each other and tried to not even breathe, much less move. Then, finally, almost as an afterthought, it seemed, she came back to check on the robot.

I watched, helpless and with growing dread, as her watery eyes moved from the empty glass case to the floor, then to Gax, then to Spuckler, and finally, after a shudder of disbelief, to me.

"Take what you need and leave!" she cried, her voice little more than a whimper. "Just don't hurt me!"

No way. She's scared of us?

"I'll do anything if you'll spare my life!" Her voice was shaking like mad. The blood had gone from her face, leaving her bone white, and she looked as though she was well on the way to fainting. "I can get you money if that's what you want!"

Talk about luck. All she had to do was turn around and run for the palace guards and we'd be completely surrounded in seconds. Instead, she was

standing there like a frightened child, cowering before us as if we were armed and dangerous.

Spuckler spoke first.

"How much money are we talkin' about here?"

"Spuckler!" I jabbed him with a pointy elbow.

"There are five hundred gilpots hidden in a beaker under the sink!" the woman blurted out.

"The sink, eh?" Spuckler was already scanning the room.

"Spuckler!" I jabbed him with a much pointier elbow.

"Ow!"

I glared at Spuckler and pressed a finger across his lips. "You know, it would be a lot easier for me to help you if you could *stop committing crimes for a few seconds!*"

"Awright, awright," said Spuckler, clearly disappointed with my turning out to be such a party pooper. "Jeez."

I turned to the woman, who was, if anything, cowering even more than before.

"Look, we're not going to hurt you."

The woman suddenly stopped cowering.

I raised a cautionary finger and tried to look tough. "Unless we *have* to." (I know, I know: it's not nice to threaten people. It was for a good cause, though, right?)

I stepped forward and put a firm hand on the woman's arm, in a way that I hoped would be both comforting and ever so slightly intimidating. "Ma'am, you may or may not believe this, but this young man here is completely innocent of the crime he's been accused of."

Spuckler spoke aloud, to himself as much as anyone else: "*Completely* innocent? You know, I'm not so sure I'd say *complete*—"

"Will you be quiet?" I swear. The guy was even more strangle-worthy as a teenager than as an adult.

I sighed and decided to keep my conversation with the woman short and sweet, so as to deprive Spuckler of any further opportunities to blow it.

"Ma'am, we need you to—"

"Help you escape?" she asked, nodding enthusi-
astically.

I took a deep breath. How on earth had we
managed to get this lucky? "Um, yeah. Escape.
That's . . . exactly what we need to do."

"The royal transport hangar," said the woman.
"My personal jet scooter is there. It's yours if you
agree not to hurt me. I'll give you the key and you'll
be out of this palace and miles away before anyone's
the wiser."

"Jet scooter?" Spuckler clapped his hands and
gave a whistle. "Now you're talkin'." He bent over,
picked up Gax (whose immobilizer patch was still
stubbornly in place), tucked him under one arm,
and began strolling toward the lab door. "Lead the
way, Granny, lead the way!"

I probably should have scolded Spuckler for
calling the woman "Granny." But she did have a
very grandmotherly air about her. There was no
denying it.

"No, not the front entrance," said the woman, waving madly for him to stop. "The corridors out there are crawling with guards. We've got to get out of here without being seen."

We?

It occurred to me that she wasn't doing this simply because she was scared of us. I think on some level she actually sympathized with us, or even felt sorry for us. Perhaps she could see that Spuckler and I didn't have the vile character needed to carry out the crime we'd been accused of. More likely she just saw that we didn't have the brains. In any case, she was the first person in a very long time to treat us with any degree of kindness, and for that I was grateful.

"There's a delivery door back here," she continued, motioning us to the far wall. "We'll stand a far better chance of slipping out unnoticed if we go that way."

"Hang on," I said, placing a hand—this time much more gently—on the woman's arm. "If we're going to go any further with this, I think we should at least know one another's names. Mine's Akiko, and this is Spuckler."

"Spuck," said Spuckler, extending his free hand and shaking the woman's with so much force you'd have thought he wanted to leave "Granny" with a fractured wrist.

"Plapp," said the woman, rubbing her knuckles after Spuckler finally unlocked his iron grip. "Hwindolyn Plapp, at your service."

"At our service?" I said with a grin. "You can say *that* again, Hwindolyn. More like saving our hides."

"I haven't saved them yet, Akiko," she said, extending her hand to me in anticipation of a far less bruising handshake. "And please, call me Hwinny. All my friends do."

I tilted my head to one side as I took her hand in mine, mildly astonished to hear that she had just pronounced us friends.

"Thanks, Hwinny," I said, holding her hand long enough to transform the handshake from a mere greeting into something rather more like the sealing of a contract.

"My pleasure entirely," she said, then turned to show me the way to the delivery door.

Only then did I realize that Spuckler was nowhere to be seen.

"Spuckler!" I said as loudly as I dared. "Where are you?"

"Now, I ain't 'cusin' you of lyin', Granny," said Spuckler, emerging from behind a counter with a beaker in one hand and a wad of bills in the other, "but this is a goldurned sight short of five hunnerd gilpots."

Chapter 12

We reached the transport hangar about half an hour later, following a mercifully uneventful trek through half a dozen rooms and corridors deep in the heart of King Froptoppit's palace. (Well, unless you count as eventful Spuckler's noisy griping about my not letting him keep the "four hunnerd twenny-seven and a half gilpots" he wanted so dearly to make off with.)

When we got to the hangar, we found it only lightly guarded. There was, in fact, only one guard on duty: Fatch. Unfortunately, as we by now knew all too well, one Fatch was more than a match for the still-scrawny Spuckler. Plus he was seated,

Hwinny explained, right next to an alarm switch that, if thrown, would bring an entire squadron of armed sentries within seconds. Finally, a key on Fatch's belt was the only way of opening the exit through which the jet scooters could pass. For now, that exit was sealed by a huge segmented wall of cast

iron that looked like a garage door designed for—
and possibly by—Godzilla.

"I can take 'im this time," Spuckler said, putting
on a show of confidence. "What is he, three hunnerd pounds?"

And what are you, I wanted to say, *ninety-eight?*

Even in twenty years' time, Spuckler would have his work cut out for him taking on a guy like Fatch. For now, I could only envision one outcome: an embarrassingly faithful reproduction of the scene we'd been treated to earlier, with Spuckler reprising the part of the easy chair.

"It would be a pretty even match," said Hwinny, eliciting an appreciative nod from Spuckler. I could see in her eyes that she didn't believe her own words. She was only saying them to lift Spuckler's spirits. "But you'd better let me handle him."

"*Y-you?*" I said.

Hwinny gave me a quizzical look, then chuckled like a schoolgirl. "What do you think I'm talking about, dear girl? A crippling chop to the neck?" She grinned and patted me affectionately on the cheek. "I'm going to *talk* to him, Akiko. He trusts me. I'll tell him I need the door raised for some reason or other. He'll throw the switch," she continued as she opened Spuckler's hand and placed the key to her jet scooter neatly in the middle of it, "and you'll be just one good engine rev away from bidding this place adieu." She closed Spuckler's fingers around the key and added: "Don't worry about returning the jet scooter. They'll get me a new one every bit as good, no doubt."

How perfect can you get? Well, perfect for Spuckler, Gax, and me. But from Hwinny's point of view, I realized upon further reflection, the plan had some serious drawbacks.

"What will happen to you once we're gone?" I had a brief but vivid vision of Hwinny wasting away in the palace dungeon. "They'll say you were in cahoots with us," I said, then added: "Which, let's face it, you are."

Hwinny beamed. "And I'm enjoying every minute of it. Why, I haven't felt this young in years. You've helped me discover a whole new side to myself: I had no idea I had such a facility for derring-do."

She put a calming hand on mine and gave me a little squeeze. "Don't worry. They'll never suspect a thing. I'll tell them I did everything under duress. I'll, I'll . . ." She paused and tapped her fingers against her chin. "I'll tell them Spuckler said he's a mobster kingpin. That he knows where my grand-children live, and"—a mischievous twinkle came into her eye—"and that he'd have them all kid-napped and held for ransom if I didn't help you escape."

Spuckler gave this a little thought, then shook his head. "Naw, Granny, kidnappin's not my bag. Specially not kids. I draw the line at kids." He raised a finger to emphasize this point, then added with a whisper: "I like the mobster kingpin part, though. I got a friend who does that. Looks like a pretty cool gig."

I was about to point out that Mr. Beeba would never believe that Spuckler was anything other than a habitual goofball, but then it hit me: Mr. Beeba didn't even *know* Spuckler yet. He'd believe any-thing at this point.

Now I was the one giving the appreciative nod. "Hwinny, do you really think this will work?"

"I *know* it will," Hwinny replied. "Fatch, if you haven't noticed, is not exactly the brightest fellow in the palace."

Sadly, agreeing to Hwinny's plan meant that it was time to say goodbye to her. It was amazing how attached I'd become to her during the brief time we'd spent together, and I found myself wishing, somewhat perversely, that she could come with us.

Just before she left to get the plan under way, she turned back for one last bit of unfinished business. "Thief or not," she said to Spuckler as she placed a practiced hand on Gax's immobilizer patch and removed it as effortlessly as someone taking a magnet off a refrigerator, "you'll not be wanting to take *this* with you, I expect."

KWZIT

TH'PIP

SHPOK

All at once Gax sprang to life, every bit as animated as I remembered him. Maybe even more so: he was, after all, still fresh from the factory.

"THANK YOU, MA'AM," Gax said, bowing politely to Hwinny. "I WAS BEGINNING TO FEAR I'D NEVER BE ALLOWED TO MOVE AGAIN."

"Li'l buddy!" said Spuckler. "Sure is good to see you back to your old self. I ain't got no use for an oversized paperweight."

Hwinny and I smiled as Spuckler threw his arms around Gax and gave him a great big hug.

"Now, Gax," Spuckler said once he was done, "this here's Akiko. She's gonna be taggin' along with us for a while." He then added, in a whisper I wasn't meant to hear: "Don't worry. It'll only be for an hour or two, then we'll get rid of her. You know me—I ain't about t' make a *girl* a permanent part of the team." Gax nodded, as if he were well aware of Spuckler's policy in this area.

"An' this here's, uh . . . ," said Spuckler, evidently

unable to remember any name for Hwinny other than Granny, "uh . . ."

"Hwinny," I said, eliciting a sigh of relief from Spuckler.

"IT IS A GREAT PLEASURE TO MAKE YOUR ACQUAINTANCE, MA'AM," said Gax, "AND TO BE THE BENEFICIARY OF YOUR ACT OF CLEMENCY."

"The pleasure is all mine, Gax," said Hwinny, "but sadly, I must with this very same breath say farewell to you"—she shot a glance at me and Spuckler—"as indeed I must to the two of you."

"Thanks for everything, Hwinny," I said, throwing my arms around her and hugging her with almost as much warmth as I would my own grandmother. "I wish there were some way we could repay you."

"You can repay me, my dear child," she said, wiping a tear from her eye, "by embracing your new life and never coming back to this planet again."

Certain as I was that I would not only come back to Smoo again, but would do so again and again, I knew I ought to tell her I wouldn't be able to repay her precisely as she had requested. But I was pretty sure she only meant to wish me well, so I decided to let it go.

Our goodbyes said, there was nothing left to do but watch and wait as Hwinny walked across the transport hangar floor to win us our freedom.

Chapter 13

The plan went flawlessly. At first, anyway. Whatever excuse Hwinny came up with for needing the hangar door opened, it must have been a really good one. She spoke to Fatch for all of fifteen seconds before, clearly suspecting nothing, he grabbed the key from his belt and inserted it into a control panel in front of him. There was a mighty whirring sound as motors on the walls roared to life and the seemingly unliftable iron door began rising to the ceiling.

"This is it," said Spuckler, indicating to Gax and me that it was time for us—using the noise of the rising door to cover the sound of our footsteps—to make our way to Hwinny's jet scooter. "Hello, freedom: goodbye,

Topfroppit." (I was about to correct Spuckler on his pronunciation of Froptoppit, but hey, I knew he'd get it right eventually.)

We snuck over to the scooter and climbed aboard. It was about the size of a large motorcycle, but with no wheels, and tail fins instead of an exhaust pipe. A cool evening breeze from beyond the door filled my nostrils, tantalizing me with the thought of my imminent freedom.

Spuckler revved the engine of the scooter to life. We were just seconds from taking off. Only then did I hear the high-pitched squeal of someone asking us to stop.

"Stop! Stop! Stop at once!"

Did I say asking? More like ordering. I turned my head and saw, to my infinite disappointment, the figure of Mr. Beeba sprinting madly across the hangar floor to reach us before we could get away. Just behind him was Poog, a look of terrible anxiety on his round purple face.

"Stop! Stop! Stawwwwwwwwwp!"

"Now or never!" growled Spuckler as he threw a switch, causing the scooter to lurch several feet into the air.

F-FLUMP!

The whole scooter tilted ninety degrees as Mr. Beeba landed, arms flailing, on the very nose of the scooter and held on for dear life. Poog stayed at his side, as if prepared to catch him when he fell.

"Let go, ya idjit!" Spuckler cried. "You're throwin' off the antigrav cells!"

"Put this thing down at once, you fool," Mr. Beeba bellowed. "I order it! I command it! I, I, I . . . flatly insist upon it!"

Spuckler grabbed the steering wheel with both hands and sent the jet scooter into a dizzying spiral. We flew from one side of the hangar to the other and back again. And back again. And back again. A few times we even flew out the open door, but we always circled back: Spuckler was determined not to leave King Froptoppit's palace with any extra passengers.

"I'll ram ya into the wall, ya bug-eyed li'l varmint," Spuckler growled between clenched teeth. "I'll pulverize ya!"

"Listen to me, you nincompoop," said Mr. Beeba, surprisingly sure of himself considering the rather vulnerable position he'd put himself in. "I am not here to—" The rest of Mr. Beeba's sentence was inaudible beneath the high-pitched buzz of the jet scooter's engine as Spuckler sent all of us into a stomach-churning corkscrew.

"Let . . . the heck . . . GO!" Spuckler hollered as the scooter spun around and around and around.

But when Spuckler allowed the scooter to level off,

there was Mr.
Beeba, right on the
hood, in more or less the
same place he'd been before, a
slightly dizzy-looking Poog floating
right next to him. Mr. Beeba took a deep
breath, opened his mouth, and, with eyes thoroughly crossed, prepared to repeat his earlier statement. "I am not here to—"

"I don't care *what* you're here for, ya nasty old

ball of spit," Spuckler cried, holding the steering wheel with one hand and smacking Mr. Beeba repeatedly across the cheeks with the other. "I'm here to git yer squishy little tush off of this scooter!"

"Spuckler," I said, "maybe you'd better let him finish that sentence. If he's risking life and limb like this to make his point, it must be pretty important."

"Don't bank on it, 'Kiko." Spuckler smacked Mr. Beeba a few more times for good measure, then turned to face me. "I risk life an' limb all the time, and tryin' to make a point ain't got nothin' to do with it."

"*Please*, Spuckler," I said, the pleading sound in my voice neatly matching the pleading expression on the faces of Poog and Mr. Beeba, "give him a chance."

Spuckler raised his hand as if to smack Mr. Beeba one more time, but then held his fire. "All right, clowny face. Have your say, then get off this vee-hicle."

Mr. Beeba winced—from either the repeated smackings or the clowny face remark—then adjusted his spectacles so that he could make his announcement with some measure of dignity. "*Ahem*. I am not here to rearrest you. I am here to enlist your help."

He almost succeeded where Spuckler had failed: his words very nearly made us all fall off the scooter in amazement.

"*Help?*" I asked.

"Yes," replied Mr. Beeba, gaining confidence as the possibility of renewed smacking grew more remote. "You are both innocent of the crimes we have charged you with, for I am now of the opinion that you have been framed. The Misp, you see . . ." He cleared his throat and widened his eyes conspiratorially. ". . . is a fake."

Spuckler killed the engine, and the scooter slowly settled to the floor.

"A fake?" I said. "You mean King Froptoppit has been guarding the wrong thing all this time?"

"No, no. *That* Misp was quite authentic. And

that's the Misp that's gone missing. At some point during your attempted burglary, the real Misp was switched with an expertly crafted imitation."

Spuckler was surprisingly unfazed by Mr. Beeba's revelations. He seemed mostly interested in renewing the scooter escape, whether it was still necessary or not.

"Okay, whatever. Misp's a fake. Blah blah blah. Come on, 'Kiko. Let's hightail it outta here while the gittin's good."

"No, Spuckler. You don't understand. If the real Misp has fallen into the wrong hands, the future of Smoo hangs on the balance."

"*In* the balance," said Mr. Beeba, sounding rather more concerned about my future as a grammarian than about the future of the planet. "*In.*"

I was about to remind Mr. Beeba that we had more important things to worry about than prepositional phrases when . . .

"Heeeeeeeeeelllllllllp!"

A scream. From the other side of the hangar!

Chapter 14

Dashing over to the control panel where Fatch had been seated just moments before, we found Hwinny lying on the floor, her hair disheveled, a dazed look on her face.

"Are you okay?" I asked. "What happened?"

"He . . . he . . ." Hwinny gasped and wheezed, clearly very shaken up. ". . . he threw me to the floor. Just grabbed me by the shoulders and . . ."

VRRRRRRRMMMMMMMM

We turned to see a blast of fire from a scooter near the open door of the hangar. It hovered there just long enough for us to see that Fatch was on top of it, then blasted out into the night.

"Fatch!" I said. "*He's* the one who stole the Misp."

Spuckler, who moments earlier couldn't have cared less about the whole situation, was the first to bolt into action. He had a score to settle with Fatch, and he wasn't about to let the guy get away.

"Come on, buddy," said Spuckler, picking up Gax and tucking him under one arm. He took a few steps back toward Hwinny's scooter, then stopped, pivoted, and grabbed Mr. Beeba by the elbow. "You're comin' with us, clowny face. You know this guy's

hideouts better 'n I do." Poog stayed at Mr. Beeba's side, looking more anxious than ever.

"Wait," I said. "I'll go with you." I turned to Hwinny to offer an explanation.

"Go, my dear child!" she said, doing her best to sound tough. "The Misp is all that matters now. Catch that scoundrel before it's too late!"

We ran to the scooter and climbed aboard as Spuckler revved the engine. It occurred to me that it was the very first time—a *new* very first time, if that makes sense—that Spuckler, Gax, Poog, Mr. Beeba, and I were joining forces to become a team. Time travel had resulted in some pretty unpleasant situations, but this one was actually kind of cool.

BURRRRRAAAAAAAAMMMMmmmmm

We roared off into the cool night air, searching vainly for a sign of Fatch on the horizon.

"All right, clowny face," said Spuckler. "Let's have some theories. Where would this guy go?"

"I'm sure I haven't the faintest idea," said Mr.

Beeba. "It has never been my custom to fraternize with the guards."

"Oh yeah?" growled Spuckler. "Well, *I* got a custom of takin' folks who ain't helpin' me and sockin' 'em in the jaw. How's *that* for a custom?"

"Now, come on," I said. "We're never going to catch this guy if all we do is argue among ourselves. Think, Mr. Beeba. Where could he be heading?"

There was a pause as Mr. Beeba set his mind to the task. Sand dunes and windswept rock formations raced by us as we shot out into the Smoovian desert.

Suddenly Mr. Beeba's eyes lit up. "I've got it!" He raised a triumphant finger in the air. "Let's ask Poog."

I rolled my eyes. "All right, Poog. What do you think?"

Poog paused, then blurted out a series of urgent, gurgly syllables.

"Urzka Zurble Swamp?" said Mr. Beeba. "Surely he's not mad enough to go there. The place is absolutely crawling with lither serpents."

"Urzka Zurble?" said Spuckler, sounding quite thrilled. "Hang on, ever'body. Things're 'bout to get *real* interestin'!" Spuckler gunned the engine, hung a hard left, and sent us soaring toward a line of trees in the distance.

Chapter 15

"Mr. Beeba," I said, "I'm not sure I really want to know, but . . . what are lither serpents?"

"Lovely creatures," he said as the terrain began to look increasingly swamplike. "That is, if you happen to be a fan of bloodsucking amphibians who are capable of burrowing into a man's chest and taking up residence in his esophagus."

Mr. Beeba's eyes turned toward my lapel pin. "Heavens."

"What?" I looked down. The surface of the pin had become crackled and spotted, as if it had suddenly started to rust.

"The future," said Mr. Beeba. "It's already start-ing to change."

I swallowed hard as I began to grasp the meaning of Mr. Beeba's words.

"If the current course of events continues unchecked, King Froptoppit will be dethroned, and"—Mr. Beeba's eyes widened in horror—"the One Hundred Twenty-fifth Smoovian Liberation Day will never occur. This lapel pin will cease to exist."

B'JAM!

A bright bolt of green shot over our heads, very nearly blasting through Mr. Beeba's pompadour.

"He's shooting at us!" I cried.

"Well, course he is," said Spuckler. "I'd be too, if I was in his shoes."

I ducked as we dodged a huge slime-covered tree by mere inches.

"We got 'im now," said Spuckler. "Swamp's gettin' thicker. He'll hit a tree b'fore we do. Guaranteed."

FRRRRAAAAKKK!

Our scooter nearly flipped upside down as it glanced off a tree.

Spuckler turned his head to offer an explanation.

"That don't count. I'm talkin' *direct hit*."

"Will you keep your eyes ahead, you imbecile?" cried Mr. Beeba.

I craned my neck to get a better view. There was Fatch, about a hundred yards ahead of us.

"Are we gaining on him?"

"We would be," said Spuck, "if this scooter weren't runnin' outta gas."

Sure enough, Fatch was growing smaller and smaller. We were losing him.

"Gax," shouted Spuckler. "Hook yourself up to the tank and transfer some of your emergency fuel."

"BUT SIR, THAT FUEL IS FOR—"

"An emergency! Whaddya think this is?"

"IF YOU SAY SO, SIR." Gax sounded surprised. He was no doubt used to Spuckler's strictly looking after his own hide first. And though it was possible he was doing this only to settle his score with Fatch, I couldn't help thinking there was more to it than that.

BBRRRRRRUUUMMMMMM

The scooter picked up speed as Gax's emergency fuel hit its tank.

B'JAM! B'JAM!

Two more laser bolts shot by us, one on either side.

"No worries," said Spuckler. "He's a lousy shot."

B'JAM

CHOOOOOOOOOOOOOOOOM!

The front of our scooter exploded and caught fire as one of Fatch's laser bolts struck it dead center.

"He's gettin' better."

Mr. Beeba moaned. "Will you return fire, already?"

"With what?" cried Spuckler. "Your dadburned palace guards stole my laser pistol!"

"You're a wanted felon!" bellowed Mr. Beeba. "What did you expect?"

I began rummaging through Gax's open-topped body. "Well, there's bound to be something we can make use of inside Gax."

"MA'AM," said Gax with an offended squeak, "IT IS CUSTOMARY TO ASK A ROBOT'S PERMISSION BE-FORE HANDLING HIS PERSONAL POSSESSIONS."

"That's tellin' 'er,' said Spuckler.

"I'm sorry, Gax," I said. "Is it okay if I—"

"BUT OF COURSE, MA'AM. IT'S AN HONOR TO BE OF ASSISTANCE."

I clawed frantically through an incredible array of useless junk before finally finding something good.

"Rope!" I cried. "This we can use."

B'JAM! B'JAM!

Two more laser bolts shot by us, one of them very nearly going through one of my pigtails.

"Well, use it with all speed, my child," said Mr. Beeba. "Another direct hit and we're done for!"

"Spuckler!" I shouted, leaning forward and

grabbing him by the shoulder. "Pull up next to Fatch and I'll lasso him with this."

"Good plan," said Spuckler. He gunned the engine, and in seconds we were within ten yards of Fatch's scooter.

"There's only one problem," I said.

"What's that?"

"I don't know how to make a lasso." I paused, then added: "Or throw one."

Spuckler groaned. "Here." He grabbed me by the arm and forced me to take hold of the steering wheel with one hand. "Make sure we don't hit any trees."

"Me? But—"

"No trees!" Spuckler was already at work on a lasso, and I, whether I liked it or not, was steering the scooter.

B'JAM! B'JAM! B'JAM! B'JAM! B'JAM! B'JAM!

A volley of laser bolts shot by us on all sides. I did my best to dodge them and the trees in our path.

B'JAM! B'JAM! B'JAM! B'JAM! B'JAM! B'JAM!

One of the fireballs finally struck something.

CHOOOOM!

I wanted to turn back to see, but I had to keep my eyes front. "Are we all right?"

"It's Gax!" cried Mr. Beeba. "He's taken quite a hit!"

"All right, Fatch," growled Spuckler as he stood up straight and began whirling the lasso above his head. "You're goin' down."

I tried to hold as steady as possible as we pulled up alongside Fatch's scooter. Fatch turned his head just in time to see Spuckler release the lasso and—

FWIP!

—pull it tightly around his chest.

"Gotcha!"

Spuckler yanked back hard and fast. Fatch flipped off his scooter and—

PLOOOOOOOOSH!

—landed face-first in the waters of Urzka Zurble Swamp.

Spuckler let up on the accelerator and we circled around to inspect our captive. Unfortunately for Fatch, our first job was to save him from becoming a feast for the lither serpents: a half dozen of them had already attached themselves to his chest and were more than ready to make a happy home for themselves in his esophagus.

We all jumped off the scooter, ran over to Fatch, and hauled him to dry land.

Spuckler pulled the lither serpents off with a practiced hand ("Used to keep these things as pets when I was a kid," he explained) and tossed them one by one back into the swamp. They protested with gurgly yelps as they hit the water and swam away.

"All right, Fatchy," said Spuckler. "Where's the Misp? Fork it over, if ya know what's good for ya."

"I . . ." Fatch wiped some of the lither serpent slime from his face. He was in very sorry shape and seemed on the verge of fainting. "I don't have it. I wasn't stealing it for myself. I was paid to steal it." He coughed and pointed a feeble finger in Spuckler's direction. "Just like you were."

"The tall guy," said Spuckler, his eyebrows making an angry V, "with the black bandages and the stiff legs."

I kicked the root of a nearby tree. "He tricked us. Tricked us into chasing Fatch. Into wasting more of our precious time."

"Sleepy," said Fatch. "So sleepy . . ."

"Fatch, listen to me." I got down on one knee and placed my hands on both of his puffy cheeks. "You've got to tell us who paid you to steal the Misp. We won't hurt you. Just tell us his name."

"So . . . sleepy . . ."

"Please, Fatch. Tell us. Tell us now."

His eyes were nearly closed.

Spuckler raised an open hand, preparing to slap his former tormentor silly.

"No, Spuckler." I grabbed hold of his wrist and halted the slap midair. "He's about to lose consciousness. His resolve may weaken. He might give me the name."

I leaned over and whispered in Fatch's ear. "The name, Fatch. I need the name." His eyes fluttered open for what would surely be the last time before he fell asleep.

"Now, Fatch. *Now*."

Fatch's head rolled to one side. His lids slid down over his eyes. But as they did, his lips opened to form four final syllables, so small and whispery no one heard them but me.

"Nor . . . ken . . . hoo . . . zen."

Chapter 16

"Professor Norkenhoozen?" Mr. Beeba shook his head violently from side to side. "Impossible. The man is a scholar. A *scholar*," he repeated, as if the word were a synonym for *saint*. "We can't trust this"—he pointed an accusing finger at the now unconscious Fatch—"*turncoat* just because he mumbles a fellow's name when he's on the verge of passing out."

"You may be right," I said, "but Norkenhoosen's the only lead we have at the moment. We've got to get to him before he's able to put the Misp back into the crown of Grazz G'bah."

"You heard what she said, Beeba. So tell us how to get to Hook-a-norzy's place."

I smiled, noticing that Spuckler had—even as he mangled Norkenhoozen's name—started calling Mr. Beeba by his real name rather than "clowny face."

"Well, I simply *refuse* to believe that the professor had a hand in this." Mr. Beeba looked at Spuckler and me with an expression of great confusion. "Nevertheless, I expect we must leave no stone unturned at such a time. Come along, then. Let's pay the professor a little visit."

With great difficulty we managed to heave Fatch onto the back of our scooter. Then we all climbed aboard and zoomed off in search of Professor Norkenhoozen's place. Fortunately, Mr. Beeba had been there many times before and was able to guide us in fairly short order. After shooting over several canyons and a mountain range or two, we finally arrived at a small castle-like building on the edge of a steep cliff overlooking the Moonguzzit Sea. "That's it," said Mr. Beeba. "Professor Norkenhoozen's place."

Spuckler brought the scooter in for a landing. We had a close look at Fatch and—concluding that he would be out cold for several more hours—left him there on the scooter. As we headed toward the house, I heard the cries of what I'd have sworn were vultures. Circling the roof were several winged reptilian creatures that looked something like pterodactyls.

"YAGLINGS," said Gax. "THEY ARE EXTREMELY RARE ON THE PLANET SMOO."

"Indeed," said Mr. Beeba. "All Smoovians are very grateful to Professor Norkenhoozen. He brought the yaglings back from the brink of extinction."

As we neared the front door, I got a closer look at the creatures in the lamplight. They were not exactly cute and cuddly: their jagged beaks and batlike wings made them look more like predators than pets.

I shuddered and frowned. "They wouldn't be *my* first choice for an animal to have around the house."

"OH, BUT THEY ARE VERY INTELLIGENT, MA'AM," said Gax. "THEY CAN BE TRAINED TO PERFORM HIGHLY SOPHISTICATED TASKS."

"Quite," said Mr. Beeba. "Incredibly useful creatures to have about." He raised a hand to the enormous knocker and banged it against the front door three times. "They have phenomenal homing instincts. Sometimes their owners use them as messengers, to communicate with others at great distances."

Seconds later the door creaked open, and there stood Professor Norkenhoozen. He was incredibly tall—well over six feet—with a gaunt face and frizzy white hair that stuck straight out on both sides of his head. He was dressed in gray pajamas and slippers, and though he didn't look as if he'd been sleeping, he didn't look quite prepared to have company at such an hour.

"Master Beeba," he said. "Come in, come in. What a pleasant surprise it is to see you." He turned and took the rest of us in with his tiny, shifty eyes. "And with so many *friends* along. It's not often I have so much company." He paused and added, in a tone that may have been sarcastic: "Lucky me."

He guided us into a large hall with a crackling fire at one end and several suits of armor along its

length. Ancient-looking tapestries hung on the walls, and an enormous chandelier was suspended from the ceiling with a long, heavy chain.

"So tell me, Master Beeba," said Professor Norkenhoozen after he had settled into a large leather chair near the fireplace, "to what do I owe the pleasure of this nocturnal visit?"

There was a very long pause. Now that it was time to accuse the professor of high crimes, Mr. Beeba did not appear to be up to the task. "Yes . . . well . . . that is a very valid question. What have we come here for?"

"What indeed." Professor Norkenhoozen narrowed his already-narrow eyes.

Mr. Beeba swallowed hard and, in desperation, turned to me. "My friend Akiko here has . . . er, a question she would like to ask you."

My eyes widened. *Me?*

"Why don't you ask that question, Akiko? Now's as good as time as any."

I shot Mr. Beeba an angry glance and turned

to Professor Norkenhoozen with a look that I hoped was both kind and firm. "Professor Norkenhoozen," I began, "are you familiar with a guard at King Froptoppit's palace by the name of Fatch?"

"I may be," replied Professor Norkenhoozen. "I know a great many people at the palace. Not all of them by name."

I examined the professor's face for signs that he was lying. It was hard to tell. People's eyes tend to dart around a lot when they're nervous. Professor Norkenhoozen's cold blue eyes were locked firmly on mine.

"I see," I said. "Mr. Beeba tells me that you are one of the planet Smoo's foremost experts on the legendary crown of Grazz G'bah. Is that true?"

"I am indeed," said Professor Norkenhoozen, "but I highly doubt that this is the question you came all this way to ask." He raised an eyebrow playfully.

"Fair enough," I said. "Let's get to the point,

then. We are here because we believe that you hired Fatch to steal the Misp for you."

Professor Norkenhoozen smiled broadly. He drew a stopwatch from his vest pocket and clicked a button on its side. "Four hours and twenty-seven seconds. Not bad." He reached out his hand to me, as if to congratulate me on a brilliant chess move. "Not bad in the least. King Froptoppit wins the bet after all."

Mr. Beeba let out a noise that sounded like a cross between a snort and a wheeze. "A bet?"

"A bet?" I said.

"A BET?" said Gax.

"A bet?" said Spuckler. "Well, I'll be goldurned."

"Yes, yes." Norkenhoozen rose to his feet. "It was all King Froptoppit's idea. He wanted to make sure you were on your toes. Run you through a drill, as it were, without your being aware that it was a drill." He smiled apologetically. "I tried to talk him out of it. Said it was more than just a bit cruel, putting you through something like this, all in the name of preparedness. Still, he is the king." He waved a hand, as if no further explanation were necessary.

Again I examined Norkenhoozen's face to see if he was lying. It was still hard to say. He was the sort whose smile always looked a little forced. Still, Mr. Beeba had once told me about King Froptoppit's love of elaborate games. Perhaps this was the prank to end all pranks.

"Come." Norkenhoozen clapped his hands twice and ushered us toward a hallway on the far side of the room. "I've got the Misp locked in a safe inside the conservatory. I'll give it to you, you'll take it back to King Froptoppit, and we'll put this whole affair behind us."

As we followed Norkenhoozen down the hall, he and Mr. Beeba began chatting about the difficulties of raising yaglings on a scholar's budget. Mr. Beeba had accepted Norkenhoozen's version of events—

that the theft of the Misp was nothing more than an exercise—and he knew far more about King Frotoppit than I did. Maybe it was time to stop being so suspicious of everyone and just accept this stroke of good luck for what it was.

But something didn't fit. I couldn't quite put my finger on it.

"Professor Norkenhoozen," I said during a lull in the conversation. "Was that you on the planet Kwamp?"

Norkenhoozen stopped, pivoted, and locked his cold blue eyes on mine. "I beg your pardon?"

I gestured toward Spuckler. "A tall shadowy man with his face wrapped in bandages approached Spuckler on the planet Kwamp. Hired him to steal the Misp." I tried to stare Norkenhoozen down, tried not to look away from his eyes, though I dearly wanted to. "Was that you?"

"Ah," said Norkenhoozen, now choosing his words very carefully. "Yes. Yes, of course. That was me. I . . ." For just a fraction of a second he seemed less than confident, even slightly fearful. "I chose not to speak, so as not to reveal my identity to him. All part of the drill, I'm sure you'll understand."

"I see. That explains the bandages."

"Indeed."

"And the stiff legs."

I watched Norkenhoozen's eyes very carefully. They darted quickly to the left, then returned to mine. "Precisely," he said, forcing a smile. "All part of the disguise."

That wasn't him on the planet Kwamp. It was someone else.

"Come along, then," Norkenhoozen said as he opened a door leading into the conservatory. "Ladies first."

We all went through the door and into the vast dimly lit room beyond. It was like being inside a huge alien botanical garden. Which it *was*, I suppose, though not one open to the public. There were towering leafy plants on all sides as we walked along a cobblestone path that wound its way toward the center of the room. While back on Earth the dominant color of such a place would have been green, on Smoo it was red. Some of the plants were round and squat: others shot upward in spirals like strange, twisted palm trees. I was so busy taking in all the greenery—er, reddery— that I didn't realize we'd reached the middle of the room until we were already there.

"Ah," said Mr. Beeba, crossing to an enormous writing desk that stood in the dead center of the conservatory. "This must be where you get your writing done."

"Quite right," said Norkenhoozen. "I really can't take pen in hand anywhere else, I must say."

Mr. Beeba stroked the oaken surface of the desk appreciatively. "We are kindred spirits, Professor. I too have such a desk. And, like yours, mine is located in a quiet, peaceful spot. My little haven from the madness of the modern world."

"So where's the safe that you're keeping the Misp in?" I asked.

Norkenhoozen grinned. "Safe?" He reached into his pocket and pulled out a key ring. From it dangled not keys, but a series of tiny silver whistles. "Did I use the word *safe?*" There was now something very menacing in Norkenhoozen's voice.

Instinctively I turned one foot away from Norkenhoozen and trained my eyes on the nearest path away from him. I tried to give Spuckler or Poog or Gax some sort of signal that we needed to be ready for . . . well, *something*. But they all had their eyes on Norkenhoozen and couldn't be distracted.

Even Mr. Beeba detected the eerie change in his friend's demeanor, and he swallowed noisily before speaking.

"Y-yes, Professor. As a matter of fact, you did indeed use the word *safe*. Just a minute or two ago. When you were talking about, uh . . . the Misp."

"Isn't that funny?" Norkenhoozen grinned a big toothy grin. "How strange that I used the word *safe* . . ." He raised one of the whistles and held it before his face. ". . . whilst leading you into a place so fraught . . ." He brought the mouth of the whistle to his lips. ". . . with *danger*."

FWEEEEEEEET!

Chapter 17

Before anyone could figure out what was happening, dozens of massive plants lurched forward from all sides of the circle in which we stood. They had huge spikey mouths like gargantuan Venus flytraps, and writhing serpentine tendrils—scores of them—that shot forward to ensnare the legs of Mr. Beeba and Spuckler with pinpoint accuracy. I caught a glimpse of Gax and Poog each being swallowed up by two of the creatures before I leaped, somersaulted, and dove into a nearby tangle of ivy.

SSSSSSSWWWWIT!

FFFFFFFFWWWAAAT!

Vines snapped at me from all directions as I

scrambled away through the foliage as quickly as I could. I dodged this way and that before—

SHNUPP!

—one of them grabbed hold of my left arm.

No. No!

Without even realizing quite what I was doing, I turned, grabbed the spongy red tendril, pulled it up to my mouth, and bit down on it with all the strength I had. There was a high-pitched squeal—

GREEEEEEEEP!

—as the tendril loosened its grip for just a fraction of a second.

But that was all I needed. I leaped away, rolled, and took off running through the enormous leaves of a different—and thankfully less dangerous— species of Smoovian plant life.

There was no time to concoct a plan to counterattack Norkenhoozen. I decided that I needed to get a view of what he was up to first. Plans could come later.

I searched through the forest of plants until I

found one that was incredibly tall with big, sturdy leaves sprouting on all sides. I hoisted myself up to the leaf nearest me and began scaling the beanstalk-like plant, moving vertically from giant leaf to giant

leaf. Taking care never to put myself in plain view of Norkenhoozen, I made my way to the very top of the plant, which reached up and over to a spot very near the apex of the glass dome that topped the conservatory.

Once my heartbeat slowed to something within the vicinity of normal, I crawled to the edge of one of the monster-sized leaves and peered over it.

"Well done, my darlings. Well done." Norkenhoozen's voice echoed up to me as he patted one of the plant creatures affectionately on its dragonlike head. "Now, remember: you're not to digest them. Just immobilize them so that they can't escape. Our master seeks vengeance upon the followers of Froptoppit. Vengeance that will only be served if they are alive and well . . ." Norkenhoosen chuckled gleefully. ". . . and able to witness Froptoppit's ignominious fall from the throne."

At this point a second person entered the room.

"*There* you are," said Norkenhoozen. "For a

moment I thought the lither venom vaccine I gave you failed to work."

Fatch!

Sure enough, there he was, strolling along while munching on something that looked an awful lot like a gigantic turkey leg. "It worked just fine, Professor. Exactly like you said it would." Fatch belched loudly, then took a large bite of the turkey-leg thing. "You'd have been proud of me. I put on a real impressive performance out there." He reenacted his earlier fainting spell in the swamp: "Nor . . . ken . . . hoo . . . zen."

Fatch and Norkenhoozen erupted into laughter.

Norkenhoozen turned, sat at his writing desk, and pulled out a pen and paper. "Yes, well, they certainly took the bait. And they fell for *my* little performance just as swiftly." He dashed off a few lines, folded the paper, and carefully placed it into a small metal canister. "It won't be long now before our master knocks Froptoppit off the throne for good. And you and I, Fatch, will be among the most powerful in the new realm."

Setting the canister atop a nearby pedestal, Norkenhoozen again took the ring of whistles from his pocket, selected one, and blew into it.

KWWEEEEEEEET!

This whistle, considerably louder and shriller than its predecessor, produced no immediate effect. But then, somewhere above my head, I heard the flapping of wings. I raised my eyes to the glass dome overhead. Not more than five feet away from me I noticed a glass and steel cupola like those found in most greenhouses, with a number of its panes cranked open to allow air in and out of the room. In this case, though, I soon realized that the arrangement was designed to allow more than just air to enter.

A yagling landed on a perch outside the cupola, then darted through one of the open panes and sailed down to the pedestal next to Norkenhoozen.

Mr. Beeba said that yaglings are messengers. I'll bet Norkenhoozen is going to use this one to deliver a message.

My eyes widened as I considered the opportunity that was presenting itself.

A message to Norkenhoozen's master: the real culprit behind all this.

There was no time to weigh the pros and cons. Spuckler, Mr. Beeba, Gax, and Poog were all trapped down there. If someone was going to stop these nutcases before they took over Smoo, it would have to be me.

I checked to make sure Norkenhoozen wasn't looking, then grabbed one of the iron beams that supported the ceiling. Gripping it as tightly as I could, I jumped off the leaf and shimmied along until I reached the cupola. I threw one arm up into the cupola and felt around until I found a ledge I could grab hold of. Then, swinging my other arm around to grasp the ledge, I hoisted myself up until I was able to climb out the same opening the yagling had just used as an entrance. I caught my breath for a second or two, then made my way up to the very top of the cupola's shingled roof. All I could do then was wait for the yagling to return.

I checked my lapel pin. It was now entirely covered in rust, and pieces of it had begun to crack off and fall away. The future of the Froptoppits was crumbling before my very eyes.

"There you are, my sweet," I heard Norkenhoozen say to the yagling far below. "Quickly now. Our master must be reassured that the plan is going smoothly."

The yagling flapped its way up to the cupola and wriggled through one of the open windows. I gritted my teeth and jumped onto its back, landing on all fours. I held on with all my might and—

FOOOSH!

—seconds later, the yagling and I were sailing off into the night sky.

Chapter 18

The yagling carried me across a wide expanse of sand and narrow rocky gorges. The cool night air whistled through my hair and chilled me to the bone. I did

my best to keep my eyes open and get the lay of the land. At one point I saw King Froptoppit's palace on the horizon, but then the yagling changed direction and began heading toward a massive mountain range in the distance.

Kradpaster Shelf, I thought. *That's where the "master" must be. Waiting to put the crown of Grazz G'bah on just as the sun comes up.*

We soon reached the mountain range and descended to Kradpaster Shelf, a narrow outcropping of stone on the side of a vast stony cliff. The yagling

landed gracefully on one of several huge upright stones that stood there like leftover pieces from Stonehenge.

So this is it, I thought. *The place where King Froptoppit's great-great-great-grandfather defeated Vorsto Sloggs.*

It was a dark, desolate place, all stone and gravel, and devoid of life of any kind. Well, unless you counted a few scraggly mosquito-like insects that buzzed around here and there. Cut into the mountain wall was a small cavelike space: a hideout, no doubt, for the true mastermind of the plot to steal the Misp.

I looked at the horizon. Sure enough, the sky was already growing lighter. The first rays of sunlight would hit the shelf in a matter of minutes. Whoever the real culprit was, if he had the reconstituted crown on his head and was able to gaze into the sun with both eyes open, he would receive all of Sloggs's evil powers, and King Froptoppit would be finished.

I jumped off the yagling and hid myself behind one of the stones.

The yagling let out a bloodcurdling screech, and a few seconds later a hooded figure emerged from the cave. He was surprisingly small. He had his hood low over his head, and in the early-morning shadows I found it hard to make out the details of his face. Still, he seemed familiar to me somehow.

Then I noticed that the hood was much larger than it needed to be for a normal-sized head.

He's wearing the crown already. It's under the hood.

The hooded figure removed the canister from the yagling's claws, took out Norkenhoozen's note, and read it very carefully.

"Good, good," he whispered. "Nicely done."

The figure looked to the horizon and smiled at the steadily brightening sky. "The time has come."

He turned and went back into the cave.

I looked at the sky. The sun would begin to rise in a matter of minutes.

All right, Akiko, I said to myself. *This guy won't stay in that cave for much longer. He'll be back soon to wait for the sunrise. You'd better be ready.*

I quietly crept to one side of the cave entrance and crouched down. If I could jump on the guy from behind before he saw me, I might be able to knock the crown off his head and shatter it, just as Froptoppit the First had one hundred years earlier.

The next two minutes took about seven hours to crawl past. Well, that's how it *felt,* anyway. I kept looking at the horizon, fearing that the sunrise would begin even before the hooded figure came back. Then I heard them: footsteps.

I put my hands on the ground, like a sprinter at the starting line, readying myself for the pounce to end all pounces.

The footsteps grew louder.

Then the figure swept past me and stepped to the middle of Kradpaster Shelf. He had removed his hood now, but since his back was turned to me I couldn't yet get a good look at his face. Still, his face was not what concerned me at the moment. It was the crown.

There it was, securely fitted onto his clean-shaven head, the Misp perfectly in place and all its remaining pieces painstakingly reassembled. It was covered with strange carvings and twisting inscriptions in an angular alien script.

I couldn't afford to wait any longer. I took a deep breath, pressed all of my fingers firmly to the ground, and . . .

"You!"

The figure had turned around.

I let out a very audible gasp as I realized that I was staring into the face of Hwindolyn Plapp.

Chapter 19

Her once-grandmotherly face was now twisted into a furious scowl. Her eyes were wide open and wild, and her yellowed teeth were clenched like those of an attack dog.

"How did you get here?" she growled.

I remained silent and took a deep breath. The element of surprise was gone, but I still might be able to wrestle her to the ground.

"Don't try it, child." Hwindolyn pointed a spindly finger straight at my face. "The sky is bright. The transfer of power has begun."

I looked at the brightening sky. Did the crown really work that way? Did its power begin to transfer even before the first rays of sunlight reached the eyes of its wearer?

Hwindolyn kept her finger pointed at me and took one step forward. "Do not test me. You will regret it dearly."

I stayed where I was. Maybe, I thought, I could distract her. My only hope was to engage her in conversation while coming up with a good plan for getting the crown off her head.

I narrowed my eyes and gave Hwindolyn a defiant glare. "You've had that crown on your head for years, haven't you? Under the wig."

Hwindolyn's mouth curled up on one side.

"All of it but the Misp."

Keep asking questions. Keep her talking.

"So why did you wrap yourself in bandages and go to the planet Kwamp wearing—what were they—stilts?" I cocked my head to one side. "Why drag Spuckler Boach into this? Why not just steal the Misp yourself?"

Hwindolyn chuckled. "You make it sound so

easy. I needed someone who was not only skillful enough to get that safe open for me, but also foolish enough not to see that I was setting him up to get caught: to serve as a distraction while Fatch switched the real Misp with the fake one." Hwindolyn smiled enough to reveal a sliver of yellow teeth. "So you see? Boach was the perfect candidate for the job."

She paused, then added: "Well, with the exception of being able to break out of jail so quickly. I tried to get rid of the two of you by letting you take the robot and giving you my scooter. And that would have been that, if not for Beeba stopping you before you left." She smiled. "Fortunately I had a good enough backup plan in the form of Fatch and Norkenhoozen. They threw you all off the trail well enough."

All the time Hwindolyn was talking I was examining the crown. She had it securely attached with a cord strapped under her chin. Getting the thing off her head would be no small task.

I shot a glance at the horizon. A bright band of red was now stretched across it, heralding the imminent arrival of the first rays of sunlight. So had the transfer of power really already begun? Or was she bluffing? One way or another, I had to make a move.

"Now, *that*," I said, directing my gaze beyond Hwindolyn's shoulder, "is a beautiful sunrise."

Hwindolyn turned her attention from me for just a fraction of a second. That's when I leaped up and threw myself at her with all my might.

FUMP!

The next sound I heard was my own head hitting the ground. Hwindolyn Plapp had knocked me back without even touching me. She had done it with a wave of one hand.

"Try it again, child," she said with a grin. "This time I'll reduce your life force by half." She pointed to the horizon, where the band of red had begun to overtake the entire sky. "And when I gaze upon the first rays of sunlight"—her eyebrows lowered over

her eyes—"you will be finished. You and all the other followers of Froptoppit."

She waved her hand again. My whole body slid backward across Kradpaster Shelf, and my head smacked hard into the wall of stone behind me. I fell to the ground and very nearly blacked out from the pain.

Maybe it was instinct. Maybe it was just desperation. But something told me not to get back up.

To just lie there and stay absolutely still.

To make Hwindolyn Plapp believe that the blow to my head had knocked me unconscious.

Keeping my eyes closed, I had to gauge Hwindolyn's actions only by what I could hear.

"Foolish child," she said. I could tell by the sound of her voice—by its volume and the way it hit my ears—that she was still facing me as she said this. "How Froptoppit inspires such devotion is quite beyond me." The final words of this sentence fell on my ears in a different way, and I knew that she had turned to face the sunrise.

"Yes, yes," she said. "I can *feel* it now. Feel it coursing through me . . ."

I took a chance and opened my eyes. Hwindolyn was facing away from me. She had no idea I was still awake.

But what good did it do me? She was already incredibly powerful, and growing more so with each passing second.

I checked the lapel pin. Or what was left of it, anyway: all that remained was a pea-sized nugget of rust. The future of the Froptoppits was as good as gone.

And there, on the horizon: just the tiniest glint of gold. The sunrise had begun.

"Yes! Yes!" Hwindolyn was cackling madly to herself and making wild, jittery gestures with her arms. "Yeeeesssssss!"

Attacking her would not only be futile, it could very well prove fatal. When she threatened to reduce my "life force" by half, she meant it. And there was no reason to doubt that such a reduction would prove permanent.

I lay there gritting my teeth and shaking with frustration. There had to be something I could do.

Just then one of the scraggly mosquito-like insects floated lazily in front of my face. It hovered there for a second or two, then buzzed away.

That's it!

I dug my hand into my pocket. There it was, just where I'd stuck it back at the Mega MangaFest: Elizabeth's bottle of Bai Hua You, the stuff she'd given me to stop my mosquito bites from itching.

I pulled it out, unscrewed the cap, and emptied its contents all over my fingers. Its intense medicinal scent filled my nostrils, and my fingers soon began tingling so much it was as if they were on fire.

I looked at the horizon. The first rays of sunlight were now pouring across the hills. Hwindolyn was howling like an animal, hungrily drinking it all in.

"Power!" she shrieked. "Powwwwwerrrrrr!"

I lifted my Bai Hua You–soaked hands, palms open, and ran the short distance to Hwindolyn in a matter of seconds. She never knew what hit her.

I threw my hands in front of her face and jabbed my fingers into her eyes.

"Gyyyyyyyaaaaaggh!"

Hwindolyn shrieked as the Bai Hua You burned beneath her eyelids.

"You horrible little pest!" she cried as she stretched a hand out and shot a blast of energy just past my shoulder. It hit one of the giant boulders and cleaved it neatly in half.

She's still got power. But I've blinded her for the time being.

"I'll destroy you for this!" Hwindolyn began sending blasts of energy in all directions. "*Destroy* you!" Boulders cracked and holes exploded in the ground on all sides.

Rage had made Hwindolyn careless, though, and

each shot was farther from me than the last. What's more, the blasts seemed to be weakening.

The sunlight has stopped entering her eyes. She's got nothing to replenish the energy she's expending.

I stepped quietly behind her as she fired one last blast of energy off into the sky, hitting nothing at all.

Taking a deep breath, I tore the cord under Hwindolyn's chin and pulled the crown from her head.

"Yyyyaaaauugggh!"

Hwindolyn dropped to her knees. Her tears had begun to wash the Bai Hua You from her eyes, but it was already too late for her. Without the crown she was every bit the frail, grandmotherly woman she'd appeared to be when I'd first met her.

"Give it back," she cried. "Give it back to me!"

I held the crown high above my head for a moment, then hurled it at the mountain wall with all my might.

PASH!

It shattered into fragments. The crown of Grazz G'bah was no more.

And there, glistening on my shirt in the early morning sunlight: the lapel pin, fully restored. King Froptoppit's future was secure.

Chapter 20

I grabbed the Misp and several of the larger pieces of the crown and stuffed them into my pockets. I took one last look at the quivering, sobbing figure of Hwindolyn Plapp, then left her there and began my descent to the plains below. Since I'd seen Froptoppit's palace on the way to Kradpaster Shelf, I had a pretty good idea of how to get there. It took a few hours, but by midmorning I arrived at the palace gates. When I showed the missing Misp to the guards and told them that I had destroyed the crown of Grazz G'bah, they welcomed me with open arms.

There was no time for playing the hero, though.

My main concern was making sure that my friends were okay. When I explained their situation to King Froptoppit, he dispatched an elite crew of palace guards to Professor Norkenhoozen's place. By midday Norkenhoozen and Fatch were under palace arrest (I like to think they ended up in the very same cells Spuckler and I were in) and Mr. Beeba, Spuckler, Gax, and Poog had all been safely extracted from the horrid plant beasts.

A separate crew of palace guards was sent to Kradpaster Shelf, but by then, sadly, Hwindolyn Plapp was long gone. King Froptoppit vowed that she would quickly be found and captured. For me, though, it was enough to know that she had been defeated and could not—for now, anyway—cause King Froptoppit any further problems.

The rest of the afternoon was spent watching the Smoovian Liberation Day parade, which proved very spectacular indeed. There were enormous animals that looked like whales with centipede legs; there were robotic marching bands that played fantastically complicated melodies at incredible speeds; there were acrobats that flipped and whirled and defied gravity in so many ways I felt certain they were exempt from the stuff; and when the parade was over, there was food. Man, oh man, was there food. Course after course of the most delicious and succulent dishes you can imagine, the last of which was a very generous slice of Smagberry upside-down-and-inside-out cake.

I spent the night in a sumptuous room in King Froptoppit's palace, where I slept more soundly than I had in months (due more to sheer exhaustion than anything else). In the morning it was time to deal with the thorny issue of getting me back: back to my own home planet, and back to my own, well . . . *time zone* is not the right phrase, but I think you know what I mean. It was no simple task. Eventually it was decided that Mr. Beeba, Spuckler, Gax, Poog, and I would go to have a look at the spaceship I'd arrived in the previous day and see if it offered any clues.

So we climbed aboard a scooter and—after a bit of searching—found the crash site, looking much as I'd left it the day before.

"You're in luck," said Mr. Beeba, reemerging about an hour after he had disappeared into the interior of the ship with nothing more than an armful of books and a flashlight. "Apparently the rocket engineers who built this ship had the foresight—er, *will* have the foresight—to include a highly sophisticated flight path reenactment device."

Spuckler nodded sagely for a moment, then scratched his head and said, "Reen-*what*-ment device?"

Mr. Beeba rolled his eyes. "Let's just say that this ship, once it's back up and running, should be able to retrace precisely the same flight path it followed yesterday, but in reverse. In theory, it should send you right back to the time period you were in when you first entered the holofield."

"In *theory*?" I asked, narrowing my eyes. "What if your theory is wrong?"

Mr. Beeba narrowed his eyes right back at me. "It may *well* be. Perhaps you'd prefer playing it safe and staying here until you're old and gray."

Spuckler put a hand on my shoulder. "Don't stick around here any longer than ya have to, 'Kiko. It's a pretty boring planet. I'll be on my way to the next star system first chance I get."

I smiled, knowing as I did that Spuckler would soon settle down on Smoo and make himself a happy home not too terribly far from the very spot in which we stood. As for me, I wasn't quite ready to call anyplace home other than good old planet Earth.

I reached down into the bag of tools Spuckler had brought along, pulled out two wrenches, and handed one each to Spuckler and Gax. "All right, then. You two fix the engine and then we'll put Mr. Beeba's theory to the test."

Spuckler and Gax worked on the engine all morning long, and for the better part of the afternoon as well. Finally, as the sun began to sink in the

Smoovian sky, Spuckler slammed the engine door shut and said, "Well, she ain't no hot rod, but she's good enough to get us where we're goin'."

So we all piled in, and a few minutes (and one very rough takeoff) later, I was back in outer space, this time with my trusty Smoovian crew to keep me company. Mr. Beeba's theory proved absolutely correct, and happily, the reverse path through the holofield proved a good deal less traumatic than the forward path, if only because this time we were very careful to keep loose junk from flying around and slamming into anyone's head.

When we arrived in the upper reaches of Earth's atmosphere, I knew it was time to get transmoovulated back to Middleton. So I said my goodbyes. I was careful to spend a good amount of time with each of them: Spuckler, Gax, Poog, and Mr. Beeba. I had no way of knowing how long it would be before we were reunited. And I had to ask Mr. Beeba one very thorny question.

"Now that you guys know who I am twenty-five

years before you're supposed to know who I am, won't that alter the course of history? I mean, you'll be saying 'Long time, no see,' instead of 'Nice to meet you.'"

"You needn't worry about that," said Mr. Beeba with a wink. "I detest the phrase 'long time, no see.'" He adjusted his spectacles a bit and added: "I've got a device back at the lab I invented several years ago to deal with painful memories of mine from grade school. I call it the selective memory erasifier. I'll make sure that anyone who came into contact with you has both your name and your face permanently removed from their brain. When we meet you twenty-five years hence, it will truly be as if for the first time. And all the adventures you've spoke of will unfold just as they are destined to."

"Darn right, they will!" said Spuckler. "I ain't never passed up an adventure in all my days, and I don't plan on startin' now."

"Quickly, now," said Mr. Beeba, gesturing at the transmoovulator. "I've only just a moment ago learned how to operate this thing, and the manual does say something about—"

"I know, I know," I said. "Rearranged internal organs." I then leaned over, patted Mr. Beeba gently on his pompadour, and whispered, "Enjoy this stuff up here while you can."

Mr. Beeba gasped as he raised his fingers to his hair. "You mean . . ."

"Don't worry." I smiled and winked. "You'll look better without it."

I stepped onto the transmoovulator and tried not to get too emotional as I bid Spuckler, Gax, Poog, and Mr. Beeba one final farewell. "I wish I could say 'See you soon . . .'" I wiped something from my eye. ". . . but I think we all know it's going to be a while."

Mr. Beeba threw a switch and . . .

dup

dudda-dup

dudda-dup-dup-dup!

A sea of white glowed brighter and brighter, and just when I thought my eyes were going to be blasted right out from under my eyelids . . .

FFLAAAAAAAAAM!

. . . I looked down and saw the surprisingly welcome sight of parking lot asphalt. It was midday, and the sun was shining warm upon my skin. I was standing between two enormous minivans, and there in front of me was the Akiko replacement robot with a very confused look on her face.

"That's strange," she said. "You were only gone

for a split second." She turned her attention to the rocket ship above. "The transmoovulator must be malfunctioning."

"Must be," I said. "Tell you what. I don't think I really need to see the Smoovian Liberation Day celebrations after all." I stepped to one side and invited the Akiko replacement robot to be transmoovulated in my place. "Now, when you get up there, make sure you tell the Beeba Bot to steer clear of any and all holofields. Those things are nothing but trouble."

The Akiko robot now looked even more confused. "But how do you know about the Beeba Bot? I never told you abou—"

"Gotta run," I said as I waved goodbye. "My friend's waiting. You know how it is."

I turned my back to her and smiled at the all-too-familiar *dup-dup-dupping* noise I heard as I walked away.

Chapter 21

When I got back to the table, I tried to distract Elizabeth from the whole "Natalaurianna" thing by introducing a new subject right from the get-go. "Elizabeth, thank you *so* much for the Bai Hua You. It's incredible. You really saved my life, giving me that stuff."

Elizabeth was unimpressed. "All right, now, come clean. Who *was* that girl? And that was a *wig* she was wearing, wasn't it?"

I looked at Elizabeth, took a deep breath, and prepared to cook up some sort of bizarre but hopefully believable story. Then I stopped myself.

Why not?

Why not tell her the truth?

The very idea took my breath away. I had never told anyone about my visits to the planet Smoo. No one. Not my parents. Not my cousin Earl. No one.

But Elizabeth. Elizabeth was so easy to talk to. And she'd keep the secret. Keep it for sure. She wasn't like a lot of kids at school. She took her promises very seriously.

Why not tell her everything? Everything from the very first time I went to Smoo back in the fourth grade?

I moved my face a bit closer to Elizabeth's and stared at her with an intensity I'm pretty sure she'd never encountered from me before. "Okay, look. If you'll agree to just three preconditions, I'll tell you not only who that girl was, but also where she came from, how I know her, and . . . well, an awful lot of stuff about me that no one else on the face of the earth knows."

Elizabeth raised one eyebrow and swallowed loudly.

"Number one," I said. "Everything I say will remain—for the rest of our lives—a secret known only to you and me."

Elizabeth nodded.

"Number two. You can't at any time say 'Oh, come on,' or 'Gimme a break,' or 'What kind of fool do you take me for?'"

Elizabeth nodded vigorously.

"Number three." I scooted my chair back and

rose to my feet. "We've gotta get out of here and go get something to eat."

Elizabeth smiled from ear to ear and started loading copies of *Buckler Spoach* into her backpack. "Now, *there's* a precondition I can agree to." She gave me one last searching stare. She seemed somehow aware that the things I was about to tell her were considerably more mind-blowing than the average sixth grader's secrets. But if she had a more probing question to ask, she must have decided to set it aside. "So what are you hungry for?" she asked.

I paused, considered the options, then gave her a knowing look.

"How about dim sum?"

"Mmmmm," said Elizabeth. "Sounds great."

About the Author

Mark Crilley was raised in Detroit, where he often dreamed of time travel into the past, figuring it would allow him to get in a few extra weeks of summer vacation every year. After graduating from Kalamazoo College in 1988, he traveled to Taiwan and Japan, where he taught English to students of all ages for nearly five years. It was during his stay in Japan in 1992 that he created the story of Akiko and her journey to the planet Smoo. First published as a comic book in 1995, the Akiko series has since earned Crilley numerous award nominations, as well as a spot on *Entertainment Weekly*'s "It List" in 1998. Mark Crilley is also the author of the Billy Clikk series for young readers. He lives in Michigan with his wife, Miki, and their children, Matthew and Mio.

Visit the author at www.markcrilley.com.

Read all of Akiko's adventures!

Akiko on the Planet Smoo

ISBN: 978-0-440-41648-7

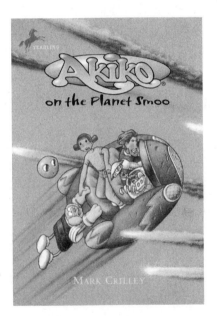

Akiko in the Sprubly Islands

ISBN: 978-0-440-41651-7

Akiko and the Great Wall of Trudd

ISBN: 978-0-440-41654-8

Akiko in the Castle of Alia Rellapor

ISBN: 978-0-440-41657-9

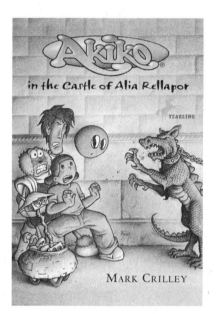

Akiko and the Alpha Centauri 5000

ISBN: 978-0-440-41892-4

Akiko and the Journey to Toog

ISBN: 978-0-385-73042-6 (hardcover)
ISBN: 978-0-440-41893-1 (paperback)

Akiko: The Training Master

ISBN: 978-0-385-73043-3 (hardcover)
ISBN: 978-0-440-41894-8 (paperback)

Akiko: Pieces of Gax

ISBN: 978-0-385-73044-0 (hardcover)
ISBN: 978-0-440-41895-5 (paperback)

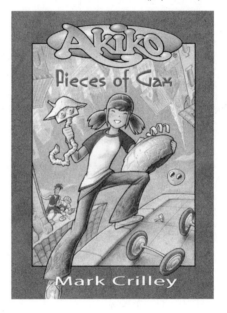